Noell & Matt
Thankyou. Enjoy (I hope)
Angela Dews

HARLEM
HIT & RUN

A MURDER MYSTERY

by

ANGELA DEWS

For

VIRGINIA LEWIS WORLEY DEWS

and

ROBERT WILLIAM DEWS, JR.

ACKNOWLEDGEMENTS

For editing and speaking the truth about the last version of *Harlem Hit & Run*, Nzingha Clarke and Joanne Dwyer. For supporting my storytelling, many, including the Harlem Writers Guild and Harlem Neighborhood Writers. And for keeping me alive and in the present, a moment and a breath at a time, a wealth of friends, many of whom are anonymous.

CHAPTER · 1

The morning is jagged enough to crunch underfoot and mean enough to explode as clouds in front of the faces of the shell-shocked where they are in line at First Amalgamated Bank, standing or sitting in fold-up chairs made for picnics or concerts or church dinners. They must have been there since before the sad excuse for daylight dawned because it's still early and two lines stretch and turn at opposite corners up both Adam Clayton Powell and Frederick Douglass Boulevards. Empty coffee cups and paper food wraps blow down the street.

And there is no music.

Winter is going to be hard again for the sun people. The wind is blowing that promise down 125th Street against the lines. The cold is seeking a way through a scarf and a collar and a hat and a hood to assault ears and to play on tender necks. Today, I would not call the wind Mariah after my great-grandmother who, although she was not particularly gentle, was not mean like this. Many on the line are her age as I remember her. And they are bundled against more than the November weather.

The boys are making us some money out here hawking the *Harlem Journal*, the weekly newspaper my daddy left me when he died, now three weeks ago. It is full of the information we have spent the week digging up about our community bank.

We got a lot of pushback over the last days as we put together the loose bits of gossip, essential insider leaks and a satisfying sense of daring to tell the bank's stories in the face of all the barriers in our path. And it turns out we were right. Today, November 13, 1990, FAB is too small to save. And we are reminded we are too powerless to make a difference.

Our gamble is on the front page of the special edition of the *Journal*:

FEDS TO HARLEM: DROP DEAD
RACISM CAUSES FIRST AMALGAMATED BANK'S
~~PROBLEMS~~ DEMISE

The paper's photographer Karl is walking the line, taking close-ups of faces. I wish I had a broadcast hook-up so they could say how it feels out loud and people could see them say it with the haunted look in their eyes. But I do have my notebook and I ask the questions, gently or not, depending.

"Did the City's only black commercial bank feel like a safe place?"

"If a new Harlem bank opens up, will you deposit your money?"

"Who do you blame?"

The next man standing on the line is mad at me. The first time it happens, it's a surprise.

"You talking about the bank closing down. That don't even make sense. My money is in that bank and I'm getting my money out the bank this morning."

"What I want is for you to be able to leave your money in the bank and for it to be safe there," I tell him. Then I turn quickly away.

"Pearl Washington, over here!"

Eyewitness television reporter John Johnson is making his way across the street. I can visualize the television shot of me profiled against the bank door, so I put off knocking and turn my best side toward him and wait for him to cross.

"John?"

"Is it true you killed Bobby Bop Nelson."

"You know that wasn't me."

"Did you forget this is not Hollywood? You're an actress, not a real cop."

How many times have I heard that this week?

"No comment."

Reverend Doctor William Garrison walks past us to knock on the bank door. He is one of several ministers who have come to see about their flock and their finances.

The guard shakes his head no. It looks like the power elite don't have any more juice than the rest of us on the boulevard this cold morning. I watch Reverend Gary assume the self-important air I find so annoying as he walks toward us.

John catches it on his television camera and sticks his microphone in Gary's face.

"Reverend Garrison! What does this mean to the people of Harlem?"

"Is someone asking those racists in Washington that question?"

"You're on the bank's board of directors. What are you doing about this?"

"Nobody's asking for a handout. The only commercial bank in the city run by black people was started by heroes and run by supermen. Pledges are still coming in. Even just now, someone pledged another two million dollars on the phone. If this goes down, then know what gets endorsed and supported is not our self-sufficiency, but our dependency, always has, always will."

While the camera is pointed the other way, I knock. A stranger inside moves aside one of the concealing shades and looks out. He is not impressed with my press credentials, which are actually expired, but he wouldn't know because he doesn't move close enough to see.

I am forced to step back to join my neighbors outside our community bank. I feel with them the weight of our defeat. We are stooped under it.

The line is a snaking thing full of stunned acceptance. The anger is barely contained in its familiar groove. As much as it feels like a unique experience, it also feels like one too many of the same old thing. Some have come with company to the boulevard. But if we have come alone, we can find comfort in the line. We are dense together because we need less personal space on this cold morning. The angry voices trying to rally us are an intrusion.

"Save the bank." The chant comes and goes. It seems to take too much voice.

"You know you aren't going back to Cali any time soon," Captain Obsidian Bailey says from where he has walked up behind me. "And, perhaps, given what all happened last week, you might stop acting like you are above all this."

"No. I won't act like that," I tell him.

Because I'm not.

CHAPTER · 2

"Go back to Africa where you came from."

Typical. And where'd you come from, brown man? I thought as I grabbed a camera. Not because a street fight is news in this town, but because I'm drawn to drama, I love the camera and I needed to fill up some spaces in my father's newspaper on deadline day.

I had to lean out the window, my body secured against the frame, to take pictures of the beef going down two stories below me on 125th Street, Martin Luther King Jr. Boulevard where it was noisy with its soundtrack.

My pictures were an aerial view of a pair of African street merchants yelling at a well-dressed dark brown-skinned man who seemed to have lost his mind. He started scooping audio cassettes and video tapes off a folding table into a bag with one arm and pointing a gun at them with the other.

I framed the wide shot and then tightened in on close-ups of the tapes still on the table and those that had fallen onto the wide public space. I recognized some of the movie covers were recent films and saw one that I didn't think had been released yet.

He holstered the gun and raised the folding table that had been the vendors' street operation up over his head. His African fez didn't even fall off when he threw the table.

"I work my ass off," he yelled at the Africans.

Work your ass off doing what? I wondered.

I pulled back to catch the street vendors scrambling to pick up their inventory and then swung over to the spectators spread out on one wide sidewalk. The crowd was magnetized to pull bits of color from up and down the boulevard to add to its widening edges.

The kids were cheering and were either completely hidden in oversized outfits or strategically exposed like overgrown doll babies.

Their elders were not interfering, my newspaper staff among them in a little knot near the front, where they had no business being on production day.

When the phone rang behind me, I had to ease myself back through the window to run for it.

"You have reached the *Harlem Journal*. For 40 years, your favorite Harlem weekly newspaper. If you know the extension of the person you are trying to reach, you can enter it now."

Roger's baritone made the tired message impressive, but before I could get to the phone, I heard, "Peace and be strong." And he was finished.

"This is Pearl Washington. Hello? Hello?"

But the caller was gone.

Roger wrote the music for *Last Stop Harlem*, the latest of the couple of films that milked every drop out of a good idea. The poster for my first movie hung over the front desk where Lt. Summer Knight is aiming at you, wide-legged, hair wild, invincible, wearing brown leather so tight it looks like paint. She's me in my other life, before I became the reluctant publisher of one of Harlem's weekly newspapers when my daddy died.

Distinguished Newspaper Publisher Called Home — Charles Washington, November 21, 1925 to October 22, 1990. I love the language of the black press. But I felt like I was flying without a safety net without him. It made me dizzy and I was still too mad at him to cry.

Three weeks ago, each Harlem honk and siren and holler and song snagged me; now it was all a hum. Until I heard, "When I come back, you best be gone."

It was Mr. Cool and he pulled my attention outside again. I took another picture of him and then swung the camera to catch the vendors and discovered Al Carter, the newspaper's production manager, was helping gather up their mess where it was scattered all over the wide sidewalk. They could have been family—two young brothers from Côte D'Ivoire and one from 111th Street. They were built the same wiry way and had the same hair. Only the Africans' heads were neat; Al's was a riot.

The crowd started breaking up in ones or twos to go find something else to do. Except one woman who walked over to Mr. Cool to say something in his ear that made him laugh. I closed in to get a portrait of the woman. It was my father's girlfriend, now widow, Mrs. Viola, now Washington.

It had been an off-again-on-again thing, my relationship with Miss Viola, since my father brought the owner of the Kit Kat Klub into our lives. It wasn't just because the woman was only eight years older than me; it was also because she wanted to be the center of attention and I considered that my role. And when he married Viola at her house on the hill, I wasn't there. Daddy's death and our shared grief had finally made a quasi-peace between us.

In the close-up, I recognized Mr. Cool was Bobby Bop, a jazz man whose group was one of the acts coming to the big event at the Apollo later in the week.

When I widened the frame, I caught Mr. Cool with his gun out again, pointing in the direction of Al and the vendors. "You've been told," he said.

He put his weapon away and offered Viola his free hand and walked with her to the street where a red Cadillac convertible was double parked at the curb.

The driver trapped by the double-parked Caddy honked. Viola waved at him and then flipped him a bird twice as he kept honking the whole time it took them to get to Bobby Bop's car and deposit his bag of tapes into the back, and then continued honking after them while they made a U-turn and squealed away.

When they drove out of my frame, I was left with a wide shot of the people across the street, seemingly oblivious to the action, flowing along at a browsing pace, somehow managing to keep off of each other's heels and out of each other's faces. Except my neighbor Cecelia Miller, who walked like she owned 125th Street. She had accessorized her business suit with green and red African fabric folded and tied around her head. Her gelee appeared between a broken line of street businesses at tables heaped with bolts of kente and mud cloth and figured fabric from Mali. She would disappear behind a wall of vendors, then reappear again.

I took a couple of wide shots of her in profile, and when she turned to face me in the middle of the block to cross the street at the light, I zoomed in to catch her face as she looked both ways and then stepped off the curb and into the boulevard. And then her face changed to what turned out to be her reaction to something I had to pull back to include in my viewfinder.

A late model American car was careening diagonally across the street, seemingly out of nowhere, seemingly against the light.

Then the sound of impact filled the space between us. Together we experienced her being catapulted into the air like a rag doll where she hung for a terrible moment before she dropped to the dirty street.

My scream was more of a moan, while I was close, right on top of her, connected through the camera, until I forced myself to swing away to follow the dark car as it bounced off one of the large poles holding up the streetlight. I willed myself to stay with the car, shooting and shooting, trying to get the license plate, as it swerved back into the westbound lane in front of the stopped traffic. When the car was finally gone, I turned back to find a crowd had concealed my girl.

CHAPTER · 3

Then I was running down the two flights of front stairs and down the street and through the loose crowd toward Cecelia.

Two women who were part of the group ministering to her got up and shook their heads.

Her neck met her shoulders at an absurd angle, like a broken doll's. A mess of dark hair had escaped when she lost her wrap and the tangle of it gave her a wild look she never would have allowed in public, in life.

The terrible ominous wailing of a herd of police cars announced their arrival.

I had to remember to breathe. In and out. And again.

I walked closer and put her Coach tote over my shoulder and picked up one grey suede pump. The shoe was almost new. The bottom wasn't even worn.

In that moment, the absurdity of my need to take control in such an inconsequential way finally broke me. I squatted and gathered my skirt, pulling it out of the way, rocking forward. And I said loud enough for her to hear me, "Let go. Remember all this fleeting world is a star at dawn, a bubble in a stream, a flash of lightening in a summer cloud, a flickering lamp, a phantom, and a dream. Go for the light."

"What is that?"

I looked up at Police Captain Obsidian Bailey.

"Hearing is the last sense we lose," I said. "She can hear me."

"You told her to let go. What else could she do?"

"She could struggle to hold on. This is a great and difficult transformation."

"But she's dead."

"I know."

"Are you a Buddhist?"

"I'm studying the Buddha's teaching as part of my martial arts practice."

"What you said was weird but kind of peaceful," he said.

"But I'm telling her to let go and I'm not about to let go. Not hardly."

"You must realize you've compromised the investigation by picking up her shoe."

"I stopped myself from doing any more."

"Come on, Pearl. You played a cop in enough movies to know better. Every kid in America knows the routine at a crime scene."

"I think he aimed at her. And I was thinking it was an additional crime for her to be lying in the street looking like that."

"Or it was an accident," he said. And he took the shoe and walked away.

"Pearl, look over here."

Karl, a freelance photographer they often use at the *Journal*, took my picture.

"He aimed at her," I told Karl. "You'll see."

I took the camera strap from around my neck. "I was shooting a fight out the window at the newspaper when I saw Cecelia walking across the street, and I used the camera to get a better look at her. I need the pictures for page one. Can you give a set to the police without telling them you got them from me?"

"No shit? You mean to say you got us a picture of the hit-and-run car?"

"It looked like a gypsy cab. It was terrible."

"Cool." He made some adjustments in the heavy gadget and lens bag that was brown like everything else—his shoes, pants, windbreaker, face, hat.

He retrieved a little camera. "I'll trade you. It's my new toy. Easy to shoot. With a zoom. Tell me how you like it."

An instinct must have alerted him because he turned around quickly to take the picture of the Right Reverend Doctor William Garrison kneeling over Cecelia, saying something we couldn't hear, touching her hand, shaking his head.

An orange had rolled out of a paper bag just beyond her delicate fingers.

CHAPTER · 4

I saw Captain Obsidian Bailey walking back toward me and the sight of him made me lightheaded. Then I felt the return of dread as a cold rush.

Obsidian is aptly named, I swear—dark as the stone and grounded. Being a New York City policeman for over ten years and the discipline of various fighting practices could only have sharpened the special gift he was born with.

When he got to me, he said, "Come with me. Somebody abandoned a vehicle. We think it's the hit-and-run car. We can use a witness like you."

My instinct was to back away from witnessing. "It happened very fast." Then I felt ashamed of myself. "She looked both ways before she crossed the street." I started to speak, stopped, then started again. "But the car came out of nowhere."

"Breathe, Pearl."

"And she still ended up being part of this out-of-control scene. How could you all let it get like this?"

"Whoa. You moved three thousand miles away, and it's my fault?"

"Every time I come back, it's worse. Like you all just don't care."

"Is it easier to care from a distance? Coward."

"Don't you call me names. How dare you."

"How dare me? What is that? So now you've made yourself a couple of Hollywood movies, you're all indignant and shit?" Hollywood sounded like a dirty word in his mouth. "I'm sure you haven't spent time with Cecelia Miller in years."

"Actually, there's not much about me you can be sure of anymore."

"Perhaps you're right; although I kind of doubt it. We should catch up."

We traveled three blocks in a police car with the lights flashing and the terrible racket of the siren. Obsidian was in the passenger seat and another cop was driving. I slumped down in the back. There was no way not to look like you belonged back there. It was too definite and final. I watched pedestrians outside, free to stop and look in the open window as we passed, probably mistaking me for some criminal or an informer—a perp or a snitch.

At 122nd Street and Frederick Douglass, just south of the precinct, I panicked when the door handles inside didn't work. I thought the officer was moving slower than necessary as she climbed from the driver's seat and opened my door from outside. The little smile she gave me confirmed it. She was enjoying my panic.

"Captain?" Two of the police people paused just long enough to see if Obsidian wanted anything. About a dozen others buzzed around the car cordoned off with yellow crime-scene tape. The front door was open and the radio was on, but the driver was nowhere.

Up close, it was unremarkable—one of the late-model American cars with the "T" license plates prowling the city for fares their fat yellow cousins won't take. One headlight was busted and loosened from the metal frame, which was broken into jagged pieces and hurt me to look at. I hoped the big disgusting dent in the front was from hitting the pole.

"That's the car. He had no business being on the downtown side of the street. He hit her on purpose. Otherwise, why didn't he stop?" I asked Obsidian.

"There are a dozen reasons why people don't want to stop and talk to the police."

"Don't patronize me." I hate that.

"Does it help to get mad at me?" he asked. "Go ahead. I can take it."

While I was the subject of his attention, his eyes with those incredible clear whites never left mine.

"Can you find out what happened?" I asked him. My question skirted what I really wanted to know which was more like, 'Can you fix it?'

"Somebody in this crowd saw something. We'll get to it. But first I need you to give Detective Stanley your statement. Stanley! Get Pearl here to draw a picture. She has an incredible visual memory."

"If you have the car, can you get Ceel off the street?" I asked.

"The medical examiner is taking her now. I'll call you later."

It didn't take long to tell the officer almost everything I knew. She probed and asked the right questions and took me back to what I was watching from my window when Cecelia was hit. I sketched a kind of storyboard for her with arrows pointing to where the car could have come from and where it went. What I didn't do was tell her about the pictures. They were redundant anyway because what they showed was the car and the police already had the car. And I didn't want to risk having the pictures called evidence so I wouldn't be able to publish them on the front page of the paper.

The paper!

Damn. I had forgotten all about my inheritance while I was running around outside, and I could hear the voices of my father and my grandfather in my head. They were both more than capable of haunting a sister.

CHAPTER · 5

I walked back from the precinct to 125th Street where it was even more crowded than usual with the people rushing up to learn whether it was one of theirs who had died that morning. Once they were reassured, they settled down into conversation.

I took a pencil from the twist of my hair and took out my notebook and my mirror. I needed to make sure I hadn't messed up the "do" because, even though I was downplaying the movie star bit, I was still vain enough to care. Plus, presentation helps Harlem take me seriously and I needed to do some reporting.

What I heard was that we were all outraged, shit is out of control and, although no one saw the driver, everyone had a theory. New Yorkers will make up a story rather than send you away empty-handed. I wrote down why people thought she might have been hit on purpose or why she was so careless, and occasionally some quote they had been meaning to get into the newspaper about the ongoing plot against us.

A vision emerged moving through them from the direction of the Adam Clayton Powell Jr. State Office Building. It was Cecelia's mother Elizabeth Miller. She leaned heavily against the support of Marcus Bell, dapper as ever, wearing a fedora, his navy suit hanging loose on his lanky frame. She kept dipping, and the cane which was usually enough to keep her moving through Harlem's streets, kind of dragged along.

There was a terrible moment when she walked up to the roped-off accident scene and stood frozen at the place where her daughter died, now empty. Mister Bell bent to gather her into an embrace and rocked with her long enough until they shimmered. I looked away to give them some privacy.

When he released Mrs. Miller, Mr. Bell took a handkerchief from the pocket of his jacket and dabbed at her eyes and cheeks. Then he wiped his own face. "I'll be calling you baby," he said, and he placed her gently into a police car.

Reverend Garrison walked up beside me.

"It is inconceivable she could be lying there dead in the street," he said. "Even after having seen her, I still cannot believe it."

"I'm so sorry, Gary," I said. "I saw it from the window. It was terrible."

"How could such a thing happen?" he asked. It was the age-old question. But the reverend didn't have an answer yet the morning his girl was lying dead in the street.

We walked together to the police car and I put my hand on the window.

"I have Cecelia's bag," I said and handed it in to her mother. "Is there anything you need? Can I help you do anything? Should I call someone?" They were all good questions and they sounded absurd and inadequate. She reached out and held my hand in both of hers.

"No, dear. Thank you, Pearl. No."

"I'm so sorry."

"I know you are," she said and let my hand go to take the hand Gary offered.

He was perfectly creased, his suit and shirt shades of gray. His yellow bow tie was one startling departure from gray decorum and the pointed van dyke beard a second. I hate those little beards.

She said, "What are we going to do Gary? What will we do without her?"

She broke my heart. But, I stepped back to what I determined was a respectful distance while the reverend offered the platitudes of devotion and consolation his tribe dispenses at those times. I took a picture of them with Karl's little compact camera. Being a reporter is no joke.

When the police car drove Mrs. Miller away, Gary and I walked over to Mister Bell.

His skin was dark and rich. And his face was full of horrible grief.

"Mister Bell," I said, "I'm so sorry. You were probably the last person to spend time with Cecelia. She had oranges in a bag. She must have bought them from you at the bookstore this morning."

"Yes. She bought two oranges from me. Always does in the morning. Always did. Loved oranges since she was a little girl."

"Can you tell me anything else I can use for the story I'm writing?"

"Not today, Pearl. Not now." He was close enough for me to smell the grassy smoke smell of Vetiver, same as Daddy, his friend, always wore. "And not here."

Gary interrupted. "If you witnessed something, you must tell it."

"I didn't see doodley squat," Mr. Bell said. "Not doodley I'm going to tell you."

"That's not fair," Gary said. "Especially not now. You know it's not fair."

"I know you're a selfish son of a bitch."

"We should be able to share what we loved about her. She wouldn't want us to be fighting," Gary said.

"It's a little late for you to be worrying about Cecelia. And I don't think you know what she would want," Mister Bell said. "Or care."

Gary said, "The great tragedy is that we will not now be able to get to the truth behind the lies and innuendo surrounding Cecelia's relationship with the bank and with the people who love her."

Mister Bell's voice was a croak, "No. The great tragedy is Cecelia is dead. This is not about you."

Reverend Gary shifted back and forth on his wingtips, and for a minute it looked like he was going to cry. It was unsettling and unexpected. Then he turned around and walked away, uncharacteristically sunken in the perfect fit of his beautiful grey chalk stripes. His briefcase hung from one hand and the perfect pocket handkerchief in the other hand was seemingly being used for more than decoration.

"What was that about? Another story for the paper?"

"I've got nothing for you now," Mister Bell said. And he turned away.

"I saw it from the window," I told him. "And I'm not convinced the car didn't hit her on purpose."

He turned back to me. Paused. Then he turned again. I caught up and walked away with him and only glanced up at the open window where my responsibility was waiting.

CHAPTER · 6

I followed Mister Bell through the walls of vendors standing close, their tables almost touching, taking up most of the sidewalk space on 125th Street, creating a bazaar.

On the table in front of his bookstore, red, black and green liberation flags flapped on little sticks among the sale books and videocassettes placed to lure the sidewalk traffic inside. A campaign poster for the incumbent in last season's Democratic primary was incongruous beside the perennial Marcus Garvey poster propped up on the second table behind an inventory that included apples and oranges (5/$1) and handful bags of nuts and raisins ($1).

His bookstore was one of the storefronts at the base of the Theresa Hotel where it moved when the State Office Building took its catty-corner site on Seventh Avenue.

It's the Speakers Corner, the African Square, where Malcolm, Fidel, our local Kenyatta and President Nelson Mandela have come and gone. Gil Scott-Heron offered "The Revolution Will Not Be Televised" as part of the morning's soundtrack.

Mister Bell made his way slowly through the small crowd who hover around his store like tick birds at some Serengeti watering hole. They slapped his shoulder and murmured things I couldn't hear before he escaped into his bookstore.

"Pearl, I ain't seen you in a minute," one of the crowd outside said to me. "I heard you was putting out your daddy's paper since he passed."

My memory served up the name of a slight built man, to match with the familiar face. "Yes, Riley. Yes, I am. But I'm going back to California this weekend."

"I miss Charlie."

"Thank you. I miss him too." And I did. At that moment, away from the office and the responsibility, I missed my father like a little girl.

This was his world but I had a place in it we made together when I walked around Harlem with my hand in his hand.

"Man, gimme some grapes," a customer said, and the light caught his pinky ring as he peeled a five from a money clip.

"He don't sell grapes. Don't you know there's still a boycott?" another man told the customer.

I recognized Joseph, another of my father's cronies who he argued with while I listened and learned.

"That ain't got nothing to do with me. Give me an orange then."

After he made the sale, Joseph and I watched the customer navigate the crowded street.

Joseph turned to me. "Pearl, you need to tell the story about this mess in the streets."

"Come on," Riley said. "You know you shop out here."

"I do not," Joseph said. "And this chaos makes it impossible for legitimate businesses to get the bank assistance and customers we need to exist."

"If the bank told you that lie, then why'd they give a loan to the white man and his franchise?" Riley asked.

I pulled out my notebook. "Are any of those so-called legitimate businesses black?" I asked. "Because this street bazaar certainly is."

"Pearl, I see you're taking notes," Joseph continued. "I'm telling you. There are a lot of us, and there should be more. Especially in the second-floor offices and down the avenues." He got louder. "No one but niggers would put up with this bullshit."

"What about the street vendors in Chinatown? And what about Washington Heights and Flushing?" I asked.

Joseph said. "They own the inside business and the outside business."

"Okay. And who would the *Journal* reporters talk to for a bank story?" I asked.

"Cecelia would have been good. She was a bank officer. But she's gone," Joseph said. "Reverend Gary is on the board. But he's not going to talk to any reporters about anything but his self."

"You can mourn her," said a woman standing at the edge of the group. "In fact, I'll mourn her myself because nobody deserves to die in the street. But God don't love ugly. She had the nerve to tell me the bank was not in the social work business when I applied for a business loan."

"Do you think it's fair to take it personally?" I asked her. "A bank officer's job is to say no sometimes."

"I've heard I could have got my loan if I'd had the right friends."

"Can you tell me who the *Journal* should talk to about the bank's lending policies? The reporters don't have to use the name."

"I'll have to think about it."

When I went inside Freedom Books, Mister Bell wasn't in front and I called to him at the door of his back-office sanctuary. He told me to wait and I sat down in the corner in the rocker where I always sat, surrounded by books from floor to ceiling on all sides, with the overflow spilling onto tables and stacks on the floor. But I remained poised at the edge of my seat, vigilant, to keep from losing myself in the warring upset and comfort of being in this familiar space with this man who reminded me so much of my father.

When he came out, I stood up and asked him, "Do you need anything? Can I do something?"

"There's nothing I want that anybody can give me now," he said.

He waited for me to follow him and when we were in front of the bookstore, he hugged me and then started preaching.

"Why don't the Man stop people from speeding through here like fools? Because they are white people. They are running over the bridge, trying to get out of Harlem before they get caught in the dark. Like *Night of the Living Dead*."

I heard him behind me as I started back to the office. He was husky at first but then he pitched his voice to carry beyond the crowd and Taj Mahal singing "St. Kitts Woman" over the speakers.

"Our women and children are on these streets."

CHAPTER · 7

I stopped to watch a brother dancing alone in front of Bobby's Happy House record store to Sam Cooke singing "Another Saturday Night." But I only watched a few moves before I maneuvered through the folks coming and going to the places 125th Street, Main Street Harlem U.S.A., would take them. It offered a sensory overload. I took some notes because the details needed to be captured in my notebook.

First sounds. I was aware of sounds landing—of the horns and the persistent beat from sidewalk boom boxes and radios in cars speeding across 125th Street to the bridge in the east. Offering a kind of background music on the street, Hammer told us "U Can't Touch this" and Madonna was "Voguing." But there were also the sounds of folks preaching on several sidewalk spaces.

"Jesus was blacker than me. It's in the Gospels. It says he was wooly-headed, as if burnt in a fire." They were a men-only crowd I didn't remember seeing the last time I was home. They were dressed for war, in boots and belts and crowns. They were shouting into microphones and videotaping themselves. They warned the brothers to go home because their wives were in bed with other men. They predicted the end of the world and called the shoppers "niggers" or "devils," depending. Theirs was a spooky and deep theology they assaulted us with.

"Something to read today?" The Jehovah's Witnesses were still there, occasionally trying to interest one of the passersby in *Awake* or *The Watchtower*. But mostly they talked to each other—preaching to the choir.

"My brother, read the good word. Minister Louis Farrakhan has said Allah made the black man. It was the white man who made the nigger." The Muslims were a familiar presence, fishing for converts, clean in bow ties, hawking the *Final Call* and stopping anyone, especially men, to talk about it. They sell half a million copies and could not be distracted from their mission like some other newspaper people I know.

I even pulled apart the smells: incense, aftershave, perfume, grilled meat and the exhaust from cars and trucks. It was an indulgence, since smells only figured in the rare newspaper piece about the sewage treatment plant or the herds of diesel buses.

CHAPTER · 8

When I got back to the office, the staff was in the middle of production day and Samantha was action central, answering phones and collecting envelopes.

I had finished my short publisher's letter promising a series about the vendors and was pulling together the details of my hit-and-run story when Sam announced on the intercom, "There's someone to see you, Boss."

Boss. I was getting a lot of that sarcastic attitude. But when I got to the front office, I discovered Samantha was announcing Mister Bell. I didn't expect him, and I talked to him as I walked to him.

"I'm surprised, Mister Bell. Please come in. I hope this means there is something I can do."

I got too close and he backed away.

"Yes."

Samantha wasn't even pretending not to listen.

He looked at her. "I have a story for the paper." And he motioned toward the office.

When we were behind the door, he pulled a large manila folder from a vinyl shoulder bag and shuffled through the contents and handed me several sheets.

"Ceel left me files," he said. "She said she'd get back to me about what she was going to do about them."

I skimmed and flipped the pages. "This is a list of withdrawals from First Amalgamated," I said. "And something called a National Bid List of banks that were invited to buy First. What does it mean?"

His eyes were red-rimmed and they never left mine.

"It's those hand-picked Negroes we need to watch out for. They're the thin brown line that's supposed to keep us from acting up. In slavery days, they called such ones overseers. The white man don't even have to tell those Negroes nothing. They think of the shit all by themselves by now. They got 'em thinking community and culture isn't important. That we don't need to know who we are."

"But I'm not inclined to piss these people off," I said. I touched the names on the first page in the too many places that made my point.

"They're counting on scaring you off," he said. "Cecelia didn't get a chance to say so, but she must have wanted to alert the rest of us that these people didn't trust the bank anymore and were running away from it."

"We don't have time to do the kind of reporting we need to do to run this before our deadline in a couple of hours."

"Trust me."

"You're kidding. Right?" I flipped to a new page in my notebook. "Did you give this to the *News*?"

"Not yet. But I will if you don't want it. You know this is not something Cecelia just decided to do this morning. Somebody's going to get a helluva story."

His voice broke and I waited.

"Just now, walking in the street where she died, I felt them moving in on me with their bosoms offering comfort and their faces full of pity. It felt like a suffocation. This is something I can do."

"And this is something we can do. Thank you. But I still have to make those calls."

"Do what you have to do," he said, and he handed me another sheet of paper. "And I pulled this out so you don't miss it."

I walked him out, but he turned back. The pause was a crowded place. I could see it in his eyes. "You say someone might have hit her on purpose. If it's true, it's because of this. Be careful. It could be dangerous."

"I'll be okay," I told him.

"I feel like I should have protected her," he said. "When Ceel was a little girl, Elizabeth always counted on me to do that. But this time I didn't know from what."

"I'm so sorry Mister Bell."

I walked him to the door, and on the way back into my office I touched two fingers to my lips for Samantha.

The names on the withdrawal lists were mostly the same players who were handling things when I left Harlem to make the *Summer Knight* movies. Among them were some not-for-profits and development agencies, some of our electeds, some of our reverends—and my father.

On the last list, Mister Bell gave me so I wouldn't miss it were the earlier withdrawals that gave my father his place where he belonged—in the middle of things. Substantial withdrawals were made before he died. There it was: *The Harlem Journal.* He all but closed that account.

Then I got mad. As he would have said, now, there was a fire on the mountain.

CHAPTER · 9

I told Adrianne, the paper's current editor, I had a briefing to give her at the copy machine.

"This better be good. I've got work to do," she said.

"It is. But you need to tell me how good."

When I handed her the first copy, she said, "I must remind you this infighting at the bank has been going on for some time. Cecelia has been giving Sam bits for her society column. But your father usually wouldn't let me use the best stuff. He said the bank's new president needed room to find his way and make his changes."

I waited while she read. "Damn. This is good," she said.

"Give me some of these lists to call when you get it sorted out," I said.

"Damn straight. You're going to call the A-list. Charlie Washington's movie star kid will get the newspaper inside some of these offices where the rest of us can't go. I'll give you the questions you need to ask."

The ego that attached me to my newspaper must have put a face on me.

She cleared her throat.

"Not that you don't know what to ask, but you haven't been here reporting for several years. There are some new contexts you wouldn't know about."

"Okay. While you're doing that, I'm going to write a eulogy. I saw Cecilia get hit and I've got pictures."

"Just make it short. This ain't the *New York Times*."

"It sure the hell ain't," I said. "But, Adrianne, you'll see, there is a hell of a story you can report using the bank information. And I think it makes sense for me to report about how we got the information. In fact, dividing the story between us will keep it clean. We can leave the conjecture to Samantha's gossip column. And you all are going to have plenty to do next week. I don't see any list of loans."

I tried to say it in a way that wouldn't set her off.

It set her off.

"You have a helluva nerve. News judgment isn't something that passes down through the genes. And I know you need to get out of the way and let people who know how to do it run this newspaper, or you'll be lucky to get ads for some of those raised-from-the-dead mystics."

When she turned and left the office, I could hear her heels clicking against the tiled corridor. She was probably on her way to the Candlelight III, the bar down the avenue, and would be back to work with a vengeance, propelled by jet fuel. So what? I certainly didn't drive her to drink.

Samantha was watching with a straight face but dancing eyes.

"How's your gossip column coming?" I asked her. "And what's all this paper? I thought you just listen at doors and sit in bars to get the stuff you use."

"It's a society column. And I'm not above catching the news on the fly. But writing *Kiss and Tell* is like making greens. You can't imagine how much information it takes to come up with those little bits of news."

Readers called *Kiss and Tell, by Sam,* her silly column of social events and name dropping, *"What the Hell?"* because inevitably, when reading, you'd find yourself saying, What the hell . . . I thought so and so was dead, or I thought they would be up to something else by now, or What the hell are those two doing together?

"This just turned into news," she said with a gotcha voice. "Cecelia and Reverend Garrison broke up."

"That doesn't even sound like good gossip. But I've got a quote for you." I read from my notebook: "The great tragedy is that we will not now be able to get to the truth behind the lies and innuendo surrounding Cecelia's relationship with the bank and with the people who love her."

"Thanks. That's a good one. I'll add the quote." She was beaming. It takes a gossip columnist to love bad news as much as Samantha does.

"And there's also this." Samantha held up an artist's rendering. "They're going to build a movie theater on 125th Street."

"Where on 125th?"

"Either Eighth or Lenox. There's some confusion. Mostly I'm hearing Eighth, Frederick Douglass Boulevard."

"Your society column is where your movie theater belongs. I've seen drawings for years of glitzy towers in Harlem and they never got built."

"The drawing will look good on the page," she said.

When Adrianne returned, she headed to the back without a word. I saw her through the open door.

CHAPTER · 10

I got to see what Adrianne could do when she was fired up. She and Al had made the front page a beautiful thing.

BANK INSIDERS WITHDRAWING $$$

Over the last two weeks, large withdrawals have been made from First Amalgamated Bank by a Who's Who in Harlem and Bedford Stuyvesant. Among them are some of the organizations and institutions getting ready for the latest so-called "Harlem Renaissance." And the list includes the late publisher of this newspaper.

We ask why our leaders failed to alert the rest of us to their concerns if those concerns are compelling enough to cause them to desert the bank?

One such concern is a National Bid List of 61 banks across the country that the Comptroller of the Currency has invited to buy First Amalgamated Bank. The Journal has obtained a copy.

Bank board member Reverend William Garrison, when asked what it meant, offered: "No Comment."

"Al?" I called out to my production manager who was wearing headphones.

When he didn't turn around, I walked along the long drafting table that stretches down one side of the suite's largest room and waited for him to finish making a cut with the mat knife. Then I nudged his arm and handed him the disk. "I've got a publisher's letter and a front-page story for you to lay out."

He took off the headphones and asked, "Why don't you do it? I've got some ads to do."

I could have laid them out. I grew up in that room and not enough had changed in the three years I'd been away for my expertise to be out of date. The only job I never learned was publisher.

He stood up. "Mind?" And he carefully slipped the headphones over my hair.

It was good riding on that beat for a minute, and I shook myself loose from the vague regret when I had to give the music back.

"What is it?"

"It's a tape from a live concert. One of the ones we could salvage after Bobby broke up the table."

"Did the vendors give it to you for helping them? I was wondering what you were doing down there?"

He laughed. "Look over here," he said and we walked over to a page in the train of double pages.

JAZZ MAN BOBBY BOP DESTROYS BOOTLEG TAPES

He was using my picture of Mr. Cool Bobby Bop holding the vendors' table above his head. I skimmed the story. The musician was driving by and heard the sound of his music coming from a boom box on their folding table. He jumped out of his fancy red Cadillac and shut their business down.

"Your man obviously didn't appreciate those African brothers stealing his music."

"They are selling my product," he said. "That was his concert you were listening to. That's something else I do. And it's not exactly stealing."

Al took my disk and printed my stories and clipped them to the dummy.

MILLER REVEALS BANK BIZ
FROM BEYOND THE GRAVE

A package was delivered to the Harlem offices of this newspaper within hours of the hit-and-run death of First Amalgamated Bank officer Cecelia Miller. In it was a sheath of documents about the bank. And it included lists of bank customers who had hit the bank to their advantage and were seemingly running for cover now.

We usually do not use so-called "leaks" that would tell only one side of a story because they are at least biased, and sometimes outright lies. But Miller's bank story became news when we uncovered some secondary source affirmations.

One of my disturbing photos was perfect for my other story.

Cecelia Miller
Possible Victim of Vehicular Homicide
April 12, 1950—November 6, 1990

Harlem native Cecelia Miller died after a hit-and-run driver mowed her down on 125th Street late Wednesday morning.

Witnesses say Miller looked both ways before she stepped off the sidewalk and the cold-hearted driver knocked her into the air and left her lying in the dirty street. Marcus Bell from Freedom Bookstore said, "She bought two oranges from me. Always does in the morning. Always did. Loved oranges since she was a little girl."

One witness said it looked like the car might have been aiming at her. The much-loved lady was declared dead on-site by paramedics who rushed to the scene from St. Luke's-Roosevelt Hospital.

The driver deserted the car around the corner and fled on foot. Police have not made an arrest. [continued on P_]

I had slipped reluctantly, but easily, into my place at the paper and the rhythm and pop of its language. To write the part of Cecelia's story continuing inside, I got to talk about her with the people she went to church with and socialized with at the 100 Black Women, the Links, and her Democratic club.

I was not always the one who broke the news either. Bad news travels fast, especially on one-two-five.

After the printers picked up the paper, I saw a man through the glass door at the front office. He was well dressed and good looking, like a banker I thought, with some papers in his hand.

"Can I help you?"

"Are you Pearl Washington?"

"Yes." Although something about him made me want to say no.

"Please sign here indicating you received this."

"Received what? You don't look like the post office. What are you, some kind of process server?'

"This is a cease-and-desist order from First Amalgamated Bank."

"I don't think I want to sign this."

"You don't have to. It's been served. But will you?"

I looked at Al, who had walked up. He shrugged. And I didn't sign.

I watched the man walk toward the elevator while I called Daddy's lawyer Attorney Robinson from the front office phone. He said, "I'm surprised. This does make the bank stories you've been reporting seem more likely."

"It may not be legit. I've never seen a process server as well dressed as he was. And the newspaper hasn't yet hit the street."

"But you all have been calling all over town. Bring it over tomorrow and I'll look at it."

I told Al, "Maybe you should publish the cease-and-desist in the next edition. This means they have something to hide."

CHAPTER · 11

Adrianne, Al and I took a gypsy cab to the Kit Kat Klub. Viola's club up the hill was a little hole in the wall with live music and a killer jukebox, and it had been one of Daddy's favorites. But the vibe had definitely changed since the last time I was there. It was charged with anticipation.

Dinah Washington was singing "What a Difference a Day Makes."

Bobby Bop's picture was on the sandwich board outside the Kat that night.

Al did the glad-hand, brother hugs as he walked the length of the bar, and he stopped and watched Bobby Bop putting the saxophone's neck strap around his beautiful sweater. It looked like an Armani. Al let him finish putting the neck on the body and the reed on the mouthpiece before he walked over.

"I will say you have a hell of a nerve young blood," Bobby Bop said when he saw Al.

"I'm Al Carter and I came to say I love your music."

"That's why you chose to steal it and sell it on the street," the jazz man said.

"I play. I don't want to be your enemy. I play."

"What do you play besides copy machines."

"Drums."

"Everybody thinks they can play drums."

"I can't wait to play," Al said and fingered his stick bag.

"You would have to play your ass off to make up for this morning."

"I do."

I left them to it and walked to the bar where customers were two-deep. The lucky ones were perched on tall chairs with backs, and the regulars had their names on some of them, lettered professionally, worthy of the professional drinkers who earned them. Some of the overflow sat on stools, including what looked like a gaggle of tourists trickling in to mix with the regulars.

There was a poster-sized picture of my father with hand-written messages all over it. Smaller posters of jazzmen and women darkened the windows. Balloons in the black and purple colors of mourning bounced over the bar, and a banner said, *Rest in Peace Charles.*

Even as Adrianne was sliding onto her stool, the bartender handed her a drink, which had to be the usual. My editor had turned into Miss Personality, laughing, playing the phrase games, swinging a leg, lighting a cigarette.

"Pearl, you just going to stand there and look like you at the theater watching good black people drink some liquor? What the fuck?" And the people around her all laughed.

I thought that's exactly what they looked like, one of those Negro stereotypes Lt. Summer Knight was always bouncing off of in Hollywood for laughs. I ordered a vodka martini on the rocks. "I'm taking it slow. We've probably got a while to be here."

They thought that was funny too.

Mister Bell gave me his seat and the bartender nodded to a man at the other end of the bar as she handed me my drink. "He said it's for your father."

Then she said loud enough to carry over the bar noise, "To Charles Washington." We raised our glasses.

"And to Cecelia Miller," she said.

Mister Bell took the seat someone vacated next to me. He picked up one of the drinks spread out in formation in front of him, and we raised our glasses again. He wiped the back of his hand across his mouth, acknowledging the hands on his back.

The jukebox went silent and the piano man, without any intro, started playing pretty, just running here and there, before the rest of the quartet came in with Al keeping time.

"That boy can still play," Mister Bell said. "He's had a hard time. But it looks like he's back."

We listened for a moment before he asked, "Has Viola talked to you about investing in the bar?"

"Attorney Robinson said Daddy owned part of the bar. I'm surprised."

"Vy needed some money and Charlie wouldn't just give it to her. And he was not a passive partner. Viola was a kind of connection, a kind of harmonic, to the music he loved. She could use your help."

"I don't know anything about running a bar."

"That's not all the help she needs." He looked around. "She should be here. I've not been able to get hold of her for hours."

"You all keep up like that?"

"Now I do."

I drank the rest of my drink and ordered another.

"Here on Harlem's 125th Street today . . ."

The bartender must have turned up the volume on the television over the bar because it intruded for the first time into the dusky space.

"A hit-and-run accident claimed the life of one of Harlem's own, Cecelia Miller. The car went out of control and drove onto the sidewalk. Witnesses say it was just lucky no one else was killed. The street is too full, people say, and street merchants who call themselves African vendors fill the sidewalks."

John's opening shot framed the shot of Mister Bell at his corner.

"I'm here in front of the Theresa Towers on 125th Street and Adam Clayton Powell, Jr. Boulevard where Fidel Castro moved the entire Cuban delegation 30 years ago when the Theresa was still a hotel. It's a corner made famous by its preachers and teachers. Malcolm X and President Nelson Mandela spoke here. Today I'm here with Marcus Bell, who was at his Freedom Books bookstore on this corner when the accident happened."

A hoot went up. "My man Marcus," someone shouted.

"Shut up. What's he saying?"

"Cecelia had just purchased some fruit from me."

"Did you see the driver?" John asked Mister Bell.

"No. It happened around the corner."

"Why was the driver in the wrong lane do you think?"

"Probably to beat the traffic. People are in a hurry to get across the Triboro Bridge."

"But he was going the other way."

"People do stupid things. I see it all the time."

The reporter looked straight into the camera. "125th Street is a crowded throughway to the highways and to the bridge for some. But it's Main Street for people who live here. Witnesses say somebody could get hit out here on any given day, pushed into traffic by all the vendors on the sidewalk and the people stopping to look and shop."

"Only black people would put up with this." Joseph repeated on camera what he told us at the bookstore. Except now we were black people instead of niggers. "They're not Africans. Most of these people are from New Jersey or Brooklyn. Makes it impossible for legitimate businesses to exist."

"We'll bring you more information as the police investigation unfolds," the reporter continued. He signed off and we all applauded Mister Bell and Joseph, the television stars in our midst.

"My quotes will get a swift reaction from the ever-vigilant culture police," Joseph announced.

"Sons of bitches used her death to make a little story that is not about her," Mister Bell said. "Sons of bitches need to talk about real people dying like they do about those motherfuckers nobody even knows."

They were quickly surrounded.

And, still looking for conversation and for answers, I took out my notebook and looked around the bar for someone who I expected would give me a good quote.

"What the—?"

What sounded like an explosion was loud enough to rattle some glass and silence Bobby Bop's horn.

Karl was the first to move and he had the shortest distance to go from his stool beside the door. His camera bag was flung out behind him and his Pall Malls were still on the bar.

C H A P T E R · 12

I was able to catch up to Karl where he had stopped on the bar side of St. Nicholas Avenue to take the wide shot of the row of buildings on the other side of the street.

"You fools can't see anything in the dark anyways," the Kit Kat bartender called out to our backs for our benefit. Most of the crowd had stopped on the sidewalk in front of the bar, safely across the street. On that side were storefronts—a laundromat, a grocery, a Chinese takeout.

On the other side, where they have stood since 1888, was a group of seven adjoining houses that made a set, their carved facades a solid sandstone street wall. Viola owned one near the end of the row.

Part of the early development of the Heights named after Alexander Hamilton, who had a country home there, they had been built to stand against anything but the most vehement acts of God and neglect. And that was probably the combination that finally caused one wall to crumble beneath one mansard turreted roof. The building continued its sporadic rumbling.

The bartender was right. Those of us who had crossed the street couldn't see much. But we could hear, and something was settling with a sporadic rumbling in the guts of one of the buildings.

When the firemen showed up, they didn't go into the building. Instead, they sprayed beams of light from the sidewalk and from the alley next door and shepherded the crowd away, including everybody they could roust from the neighboring buildings.

"Why are you just standing there?" I asked one of the firemen.

"See that X? Someone in the department painted it to announce the floors wouldn't hold the weight of a man."

I took out my notebook and wrote that detail for my story. "If you knew it was derelict, it seems like it should have been supported. What's the protocol for a fragile building? Do you get a lot of these uptown?"

"We get enough. But I'm not the one to ask about it. I need you to step back. This is too close."

"Okay. And you be very careful."

He looked at me and gave me a thumbs-up. "I always am."

I let myself be shepherded away and kept my distance, satisfying myself with craning to follow the searching lights. Karl was the only one of the onlookers who needed to be discouraged as he moved close enough to take the pictures the newspaper was going to need to report the story.

The address seemed familiar and I doodled a box around the number before capturing the other details in my notebook. A couple of buildings away, a *Keep the Power* banner fluttered in front of what must have been a campaign field office for the incumbent in the last election.

Police arrived in a herd of blue and whites with lights flashing. And Obsidian unfolded from a sleek black sedan he parked in the no-parking zone in front of the Kit Kat. I watched him walk across the street.

"Pearl? For someone who doesn't want to be here, you seem to be all over Manhattan North these days."

"Obie." I got a rush from seeing him and reverted back to his childhood nickname. "I heard it from across the street."

"Mmmm." His attention was on the building.

"And now you're going to have another vacant lot," I said.

"Not if we can help it."

"We?"

"It's city-owned. Therefore, we have some clout."

"And some responsibility."

"You place value on responsibility?" He turned back to me. "What about a citizen's responsibility to turn over documents that could figure in a police investigation?"

"I told Karl to give you those pictures," I said.

"I'm not talking about your pictures. You all have been calling some of everybody about the evidence Cecelia Miller collected about activity at the bank."

"Send someone by the office tomorrow. What police investigation?"

"We'll go to the office now."

"Tonight?"

"Yes, tonight. And you're lucky I don't arrest you for obstruction."

"What police investigation?"

"I heard you the first time. No comment."

"Is it just a hit and run or do you think maybe she was run over on purpose?"

"I don't think real reporters pull together their stories with ifs and maybes."

"Of course they do. Probably like real cops do."

"I do know there's a helluva lot more to being a cop than your movie version. Come on. There's not much more to see here."

He was right. New Yorkers have short attention spans. The group was breaking up. Except, in front of the building next door to the one still rumbling, as if on cue, there *was* more to see.

A man in overalls spattered with what looked like paint was arguing with two firemen and they attracted the attention of the police. I moved closer and stationed myself as witness with my notebook out in the ready-and-recording position to take the names and badge numbers if the argument escalated.

From there I heard the man, who was not much older than a kid, arguing that he needed to get back inside. His face was swollen and bandaged.

"You bitch ass motherfuckers," he screamed at the policemen. Which seemed like a bad idea to me. But I wrote down the quote.

Sure enough, one of the cops moved behind him and snatched his wiry arms behind his back so his jehri curls swung.

"Who you calling a motherfucker?"

The policeman's hat fell off to reveal a baby face. He looked like Tom Sawyer, but for the rage. The other cops were standing nearby, spectating. Except, one came to grab the kid on the other side and help rough-house him against the car. When he had finally been thrown against the door frame and pushed inside, the last thing we heard from the car was, "Kiss my mother fucking ass."

Obsidian promised a rendezvous. "Wait for me at the Kat."

CHAPTER · 13

Obsidian walked over to the police car and stayed for a minute talking. He was angry. I could read his body language even at a distance, even in the uniform. I know that body.

When the police car drove away, he walked over to two men standing beside another parked car. It was conspicuous, unmarked, but official.

I tried to get some reactions from the police and fire department crowd in uniform while I waited for him to come back. I got *nada.*

Obsidian was hardly better. I asked him, "Why did the police beat him up? Nobody told him you don't cuss out the police?"

"Clarence has no impulse control. But whoever beat him up did it before we got here."

"Tom Sawyer is the one who needs impulse control. Why do they assign those rookies to Harlem with their paramilitary training and their big eyes and their big guns—frightened and armed? And his partner was worse."

"Tom Sawyer? Oh, the redhead. He's new. Not from around here. The other policeman wasn't the rookie's partner. His partner will walk with him and give him the experience that trumps the paramilitary training. This is where they learn their jobs. Wherever they come from, their real training starts when they get here. And if somebody taught Clarence some respect he wouldn't be in a squad car right now."

"Respect goes both ways."

"Heavy will get out in the morning, if he doesn't do anything else stupid while we're holding him. As it turns out, he's part of the operation making bootleg videotapes. I suppose it pays better than his job as the bouncer over at the Kit Kat Klub."

"Heavy? I thought you called him Clarence."

"Actually, his name is Clarence. But lately he started wanting us to call him Heavy. And we do."

"He wants the police to call him Heavy?"

"No. I mean all of us. I've known him since he was a kid."

"I can see the *Journal* doing a couple of stories about the Harlem police."

"I can give you some people to talk to. I would actually like to read a story about what it looks like and feels like from the inside being a Harlem cop."

"Really? You want a story about how making black-market videotapes is a crime you need to get beat up for?"

"Heavy will be released. But, ironically, he's at risk of being busted for stealing movies. And it is a crime; although we usually don't have the time or resources to arrest them. Those clowns sitting over there in their jive Chevy are some freelance hotshot rent-a-cops from the coast who have been watching locations over the last few months where videotapes of movies are being made."

My feelings changed in an instant from indignation to curiosity. I could see the headline:

HOW DUBS ARE DONE

"Who are they investigating?" I asked and wondered about Al and the African vendors on the sidewalk in front of the *Journal*.

He looked at me and shook his head. "I've already said too much. Got riled up. That's off the record."

"You should have said so."

CHAPTER · 14

He walked faster and I refused to run to keep up. By the time I got to his fancy sedan, he was waiting at my passenger door.

"You are the most annoying woman," he said. "But I've missed talking to you."

I was probably revved high enough to talk some trash but I hung back and stalled. I looked at the face I could still sketch with my eyes closed. Then I turned away.

"You're not even going to try, Pearl?"

"Have you forgotten we already did try?"

When we got in, he threw his hat in the back, and when he started the car, the music went up. It was Prince. "1999" reminded me of a summer once when our spaces were filled with us loving and much of the noise we both made was laughter.

"I hate you were probably right. You needed to go to California to make your movies. But now you're home."

"Harlem's where I'm from. Home is not where you're from. It's where you're at. I only got these three weeks because my movie is in postproduction. In fact, I'll have to catch up with the dialogue re-recording for the film when I get back. People, a lot of people, are counting on me."

"Your father went downtown and did his corporate thing. But he came back home to Harlem. Harlem pulled him back."

My eyes started to fill up. Never knew when it was going to happen, when the grief would check in. But the tears still didn't fall.

"I cannot forgive him and his so-called wife for not letting me know how sick he was."

"I don't think any of us knew how sick he was. And I'm glad I don't have to take sides between you and Viola, who is his widow, by the way. Not so-called anything. I've been impressed, actually. First she took in her sister's kid and then she looked after your father."

"I can feel gratitude at the same time I feel everything else I feel about that woman, but it's easier from a distance."

"You know, you can act here. Broadway is here."

I laughed. "It would certainly be better than the Tar Baby story I'm acting in now."

"Tar Baby story?"

"I'm fighting against this family responsibility, and I feel like Brer Rabbit, who was kicking at the tar baby to get free of it. And I have one foot already stuck."

I watched him laugh by the light from the myriad scanners and indicators arrayed in front of him. I used to love to make him laugh.

Then I followed his gaze through the tinted window to the long stretch of St. Nicholas Avenue down the hill in front of us over the pulsing, lighted dashboard.

"This is how it happens," I said. "When you have all this technology, these sirens and lights and radios, and of course the gun, you're not out on the street and you don't feel like one of the people. And I guess you're not supposed to."

"One of the people? Out on the street? Please! I'm so much a part of the street there's a crosswalk on my back."

"That would mean you got out of the car. Does that happen?"

"I always did, even before I became the CO of the 28th. And we all do now. Commissioner Lee Brown and Mayor David Dinkins are taking us back to community policing. Commissioner Brown calls it Park, Walk and Talk. We get out of the car for one patrol hour during each shift."

"Do the men like it?"

"Some of them love it. I know it gets stale in the car. It did when I did it. But some of them have gotten lazy and don't want to walk. I don't think it's going to last. There's an undercurrent of resentment about a black mayor and a black police commissioner commanding mostly Italian and Irish cops to police people they fear and even hate. It also happened when Ben Ward was the police commissioner and started community policing with the Community Patrol Officer Program. That didn't last."

"Walking in the street might impress a bad apple or two," I said. "But it's going to take radical upheaval to make systemic change. I'm going to put that in my article."

"Wait! I need this conversation and anything else we talk about when you're not being a reporter to be off the record. Otherwise, I'll keep it to myself like I usually do and I'll miss this rare opportunity to hear myself talk."

"I'll listen. I've missed talking to you too. About everything. But, off the record, how can you work with these racists? Is it all about the pension?"

"Couple of things. If we didn't work with racists, where would black people work? Up north, they clean it up. But if we're inside we know. And the other thing is being a policeman does offer a good pension. It has been a route to the middle class. Sanitation is hard work and we can't be firemen. Being the head of the 28th allows me to call out the violence and disrespect. Sometimes it makes a differ-ence. I was able to direct one of the men to join the military where he might find job satisfaction if he sees real combat. Mostly we don't join the force to be soldiers but that's what they expect now."

He turned left on 125th Street and slowed down to cruise. Most of the shops had closed behind the rolled-down metal gates, dis-playing the dancing, strutting images painted by Franco the Great. Because even the whites and Asians who own the stores know it's a black thing.

Tribes of people took pictures of each other—usually all black, all white or all Asian, not mixed, not diverse. They clustered in front of the scenes painted on Woolworth's and the Colonel's and Puppy's and places to buy synthetic hair, T-shirts, sneakers, and music and the things to play it on, and in front of the Victoria Theater and Harlem's historic Apollo Theater.

"So, you know everything. Who's at the Apollo?" I asked him.

"It's Amateur Night."

"Wednesday. I forgot."

"Plenty happening on Amateur Night at the Apollo."

Next door to the theater, Hector was doing a booming business photographing tourists in front of their choice of six-foot painted velvet and canvas backdrops of album covers and cartoons. A pile of them were folded on the sidewalk. Six were taped with gaffer's tape on the tall chain-link fence along the vacant lot next to the Apollo theater, offering the ominous faces of men and the half-naked bodies of women. Tasmanian Devil carried a gun.

"You've got to be tough to ride Hector's fence at night," I said. "Barney went in when the kids went home."

"There are always young people on the street. And someone's child will get home tonight because we're out here."

It stopped me. "If your cops can see it's someone's child under his suspicious colored skin."

"Suspicious. That's the word. The uptown crews are targeting each other and they look like they're going to make some real trouble all the time. They do it on purpose. And the gangs are only one kind of violence. Don't forget booze and drugs and passion and greed and despair. You know. And this isn't Hollywood, Pearl. But we get it done. Most of the time it's nothing but stupidity. And we need people to give us all the information they have."

"Right. And how often do people in this community give you all the information they have?"

"You'd be surprised. Everybody has some attitude about talking to the police, until it's someone they know or something they want or some beef they can't handle alone. Really. You'd be surprised. And it's easier when we're face to face, on the street."

"Do you want to tell me what you said to Tom Sawyer, the rookie who was manhandling Heavy just now?"

"I was talking to the veteran. The rookie is learning. The veteran has to unlearn. This is a conversation we're having with each other."

CHAPTER · 15

When we parked in front of 215 where the paper has its offices, he didn't get out and he turned to me. "Pearl, our conversation gives me an idea. I saw you chanting to Cecelia on the street this morning. Do you teach meditation?"

"I teach kids in L.A. It's amazing how super aware they already are each day of their lives as they navigate their world. I tell them to turn their awareness inside."

"That's good. But I'm not talking about the kids. I'm talking about my people. Can you do it without the religious thing—the Buddhist thing? They might hear it from you, I think. You have chops and a persona. I don't think they would sit still for some otherworldly guru."

"I wish I could. But I'm leaving this weekend."

"You can come by on Friday as the shift changes. We have training in our roll calls. Meditation will be our training on Friday. I'll say so. It's at 3:30. They can stay or come early. We'll see who shows up."

"I like it," I said. "Very much the fierce practice of city meditation."

He said, "That's right. That's how I practice when I'm on the job. I learned to turn the energy coming at me in the street when I started fighting. And it is fierce. It's all about the energy."

"That's the language I use to lead meditation," I said. "We talk about turning the energy."

"When you teach meditation, do you also teach them to fight?"

"Roger is my partner. He teaches martial arts. I usually block the kicks, but I can't risk showing up on the set black and blue."

I got out of the car with a mind full of ideas and had to make an effort to turn my attention from planning my mediation back to being in the present on 125th Street.

The nomadic businesses were gone but they had left their garbage. There was the pungent smell of a dried puddle of piss. One of the horseplayers from Off Track Betting must have decided not to buy a burger next door at McDonald's to use the toilet. Perhaps he had lost his last 69 cents.

I went to unlock the metal door next to the building's glass entrance now covered by metal gates. "Look at this. Strange," I said to Obie.

"Strange how?"

"It should be locked."

"Wait. Don't touch anything else." He put on gloves to inspect the sophisticated lock box and pushed the door open. We found the lobby empty.

While we waited, Obsidian ranted about people not doing their jobs.

"I was making my rounds," the guard explained as he walked out of the elevator and into the lobby. "What are you doing here at 9:30 at night?"

"Why is the front door unlocked, Max?" I asked.

He started over to check. "Hell if I know. Are you sure?"

"Don't touch it," Obsidian barked at him. "What time do you rattle the doors?"

Max actually came to attention. "Always every two hours. I've been here since 7."

"Come on, Pearl. Let's get this over with," Obie said.

"The Captain's in a hurry?" Max asked me as Obsidian stalked off. "In the middle of the night? Something I should know about?"

"I hope not."

Obsidian stepped off the elevator upstairs first, with his hand on his gun. He took my keys and unlocked the newspaper's front door.

"Notice anything different?" he asked. "Look carefully and put on these gloves."

I inhaled through the layer of tension I'd carried with me up the elevator and looked from the doorway. I put on the gloves and walked behind the desk to the heavy black floor safe.

"Okay. The bank documents were in the safe and they're gone. It wasn't broken into. I actually don't think it can be. But I don't know who all has the combination."

"As soon as we finish here, write down everything you remember about those documents. And for now, don't touch anything else."

I took off the gloves and put them on the desk and put my hands up to smooth my hair in a nervous gesture I couldn't help.

When he walked over to the desk and held out his hands with both palms up, I hesitated before I let mine drop into his. He held them for a moment before he raised them to his lips, then let them rest on his shoulders, and he circled my waist with his arms.

"We're a good fit," he said.

"I remember."

I pressed his arms, which didn't give. "You've kept up your training," I said.

"I have to work hard and train hard to police these streets," he said. "And you've kept up your training. I can feel it. You're strong, tight."

"I have to work hard and train hard to make those movies. And I rarely use stunt doubles. It's kind of the least I can do to be real in the made-up movie world."

"Indeed."

I loved the smell of him and the taste of his lips, tentatively, slowly, and then, in a breath, his mouth was searching mine and my whole body was in that kiss. I rode a wave of memories on it too.

He stopped. Maybe I would have stopped eventually. I can't say. Seems unlikely.

"Soon," he said. "But we're not quite finished here." He stepped away.

I was annoyed.

CHAPTER · 16

Obsidian turned back to the desk. "Get me a light." He was in command mode, kneeling beside the desk.

I got up and snatched the floor lamp so it came unplugged.

"Here Sherlock."

But he grabbed for it before I could set it on the rug beside him.

"Plug it in." He was peering at the desk drawer. "Come here and look at this."

The rug was dirty around the front of the desk. The drawer was split at the top and splintered where it had been forced loose around the lock. He opened it and we saw the contents were a jumble.

"Oh Lord. I guess he had to search all the places I might have put the lists."

He got up quickly and went to the phone. From where I stood just at the door, I heard him say into the phone, "I want you to have the building searched."

A rustling noise from the production room in the back caught my attention.

He whirled around when I touched his arm, but kept talking as I touched my ear for noise and held my finger to my lips.

He put one hand up in a stop command like I was some kid at a crosswalk.

I turned away and walked out to the front office and I heard him say into the phone, "There's a guard in the lobby. The street door wasn't forced. It was probably unlocked with a key."

I then tipped down the hall to the production room. The floor creaked as I reached the door. From there I could see a shape revealed in the red light at the emergency fire exit across the dark room. I pressed myself against the wall in the hallway, reached around the doorjamb and turned on the light.

I heard the gunshot and, right after, the sound of Obsidian's gun clattering against the floor next to me. I was up with his gun in both hands and running for the open, empty emergency fire exit door. By the time I reached the top of the back stairs, the downstairs door had slammed shut. Good thing for him. Because I was good enough to hit him with the six-shot luger at that range. Not just because I was Lt. Knight, but because my father grew up with guns and so I did too. And he took me with him for the pistol practice he loved.

When I turned around Obie was leaning against the wall for support. The only sound the pain made was a deep groaning pushed out on each breath.

He was reaching under his jacket for the radio on his belt with his working hand. The other was dangling from his shoulder.

"Don't talk and don't move. I'll get it."

I screamed into his cop radio, "Officer down. Captain Bailey has been shot. Second floor. 215 West 1-2-5. Shooter ran out downstairs and out the back. Check building exit at 126th closer to Seventh."

I dropped the radio and struggled out of my coat and suit jacket and held my jacket against him to staunch the blood coloring the front of his shirt.

"You don't have on a vest?"

"I'm not supposed to be working. Not so hard. It feels kind of loose in there and it hurts like hell."

"This can't be happening."

"My life's flashing before my eyes, girl. You're all over it."

We were in a bull's eye of space and I told the man what I wanted him to know in case he was going to die.

"I love you Obie. I always have. I always will."

"Been waiting for that."

"This is how you protect me?" I couldn't help it, even with what was going on. We always gave each other sarcasm and laughter with the love.

"Sorry. I owe you one."

"I'll be collecting on the debt. Believe me," I said, and I had to force it past the fear.

There was a confusion of noise coming down the hall from the front. And a voice called my name.

"Pearl! Captain?"

Max didn't sound like reinforcements with his kind of squeaky, nervous voice, but I thanked God for him.

"Max. Here! Obsidian's been shot."

And then more voices were walky-talky disembodied things. I heard a siren, then another, and another, getting closer. Reinforcements had arrived. They were surrounding us.

CHAPTER · 17

Harlem Hospital was an experience in sensory overload. A drunk maybe ranted, although I'm not sure what that is, and definitely raved, on a bench in the corner where nobody was paying him any mind. He was wet and swollen and seemed to me to need hospitalization.

Somebody's grandmother was sitting slumped on a chair looking like she was asleep. But how unlikely is it to come out of your house to go to sleep in the ER? I hoped she wasn't dead. At least she wasn't making noise. Everybody else seemed to need to moan or holler about something. And, even knowing my neighborhood hospital is famous for successfully treating gunshots and other trauma, I couldn't imagine. There was too much opportunity for disaster. I kept slipping under my senses to occupy the place where dread lived. The herd of police was growing and getting louder and they were making it worse. It would have been a good time to rob a bodega way south of 135th Street.

Viola showed up and I watched her stamp in flat shoes across the tile floor to the window where two nurses sat. They let her go around to the back where they wouldn't let me go. I heard her back there yelling.

When she came out, she was holding her jacket, and she sashayed slowly now in front of the watching cops, like the point was to show them her ass in the tight jeans and the skin on her back and shoulders—high yellow, red-boned contrasting against her off-the-shoulder black sweater.

"Drop this trank. It'll help you keep a lid on it," she said in her deep singer's voice and she held the big pill in one palm. Her nails were a startling red around a little cup of water.

I felt it coming out as a scream. "A lid on what? What did they say?"

She sighed. "Honey, to calm you down. I think he's going to be good as new. You know I'm psychic." And she averted her eyes.

The instinct of the psychic? I took the pill and I had to make a fist around the empty paper cup with both hands to keep them from around her neck.

"Why are you here anyway?"

"I heard about the shooting at the Kat and I didn't want you to be here alone. One of the nurses at the desk over there is a regular at the bar. She let me go into the back and talk to them and they gave me the four-one-one. Said the bullet went into his shoulder and didn't come out. But it didn't hit the artery."

I felt the next breath calming me a little and took a few more with the same intention.

"Tell me what happened," she said.

"Obsidian said he was investigating Cecelia's accident and I was going to give him some documents she left about the bank. But the bank paper was stolen out of the safe. And whoever did it shot Obsidian."

"Bless his heart."

Hearing her say the blessing thing connected me to all the women in my life who say it at such times and it gave me my tiny share of comfort.

But then I was up, pacing, distracted by the disturbing possibilities swirling around in my mind.

She patted the seat beside her. "Pearl, you sit back down."

"Do you understand I can't just sit here?"

"Do you understand you can't do anything else?"

"Viola, do not start your bullshit. Not tonight. In fact, why don't you go back to the bar. I think I'd rather sit here alone."

"I can't leave. My being here can help both of you. You'll see. And I need to be here when we find out he's going to be well."

In truth, I know acting and her routine of concern was not half bad, nervous and full of flutter. I sat and I breathed.

"I knew it was something important when my new bartender gave me the message you called on a Wednesday," she said. "Your father had me trained not to bother him when he was putting his paper to bed." She stopped. "God, I miss that man." Her voice caught in a little sob.

"I miss him too."

Blah, blah blah is what else she said as far as I could tell. And I just sat. And I hated everybody.

Finally, a doctor went out of his way to find me and made me ashamed of myself for what I was thinking about my neighborhood hospital.

"He was lucky. The bullet is deep but high in his shoulder. I was able to relieve the resulting hematoma," he said. "We'll operate to remove the bullet as soon as he's stable."

"Can I see him?"

"Not yet," he said. And he turned back to the room full of his responsibility.

"I would like a drink, Pearl. Can I come over to the house for a drink?"

"Yes," I said because I couldn't think of a good reason to say no.

CHAPTER · 18

We shared a gypsy cab and she walked into me at the top of the stoop as I fumbled for my keys.

"I have mine," she said.

"I changed the locks."

When we were inside the house, she picked up a long-legged rag doll lounging in a basket by the door next to a small guitar.

"I meant to ask you about this doll," she said. "Virginia has been pretending Lucy's at sleep-away camp."

Daddy was crazy about Viola's 8-year-old niece Virginia. Since we lost Viola's sister to the AIDS virus, Ginny inherited a community of stepmothers but her home was with her Aunt Viola.

"Can I get you something while you change out of those clothes?" she asked. "There's vodka here. I'm sure you know that."

"But not after that pill. Make it a light one."

The creaks the old wood made when I walked upstairs to change clothes offered a familiar accompaniment, and the house announced me again when I came down with my bloody skirt and jacket in a shopping bag. But she wasn't fazed, and I got all the way to the bottom of the stairs on the ground floor before she turned from where she was bending over an open drawer in Daddy's desk.

"What were you looking for, Viola? I don't know Daddy to keep money at the house."

"You daddy sometimes brought his newspaper stories home to read. Is the story you're working on here in this mess? What is all this?"

"No. I keep the newspaper business at the newspaper so it will be there when I leave. That's important to me. Those boxes are some things I'm sending back to California."

"Before you send anything to California, I need to see what you're taking out of here and I'll need a new set of keys. Some of these things are probably mine."

"How about you don't even think about coming here until I get back," I said.

"I'm his wife, you know. His widow. It's kind of my house." I watched her walk around the kitchen, touching things. "It might be nice to move farther away from the bar. Living across the street doesn't give me any privacy."

I didn't say anything while I listened to her version of the way things were and only paused to take some slow, mindful breaths—conscious of the familiar heat of anger settling in my body, but also the awareness, learned over the years, that my reaction was what she wanted. The best I could do was withhold it, which was satisfying because I knew she hated that. But, perhaps, one day my meditation practice will take me to a place where I can actually accept the feeling but know it's not personal and watch it change. One day.

"I brought the Kit Kat Klub into our marriage and he brought this." She waved her arm in an arc taking in my house and, apparently, everything in it. "Your daddy and I were going to make the Kat into a whole new experience. Maybe you noticed. It's even more of a jazz club than just a bar now. And we haven't even made the buy. The building next door is for sale. He used to say I could be Bricktop, that diva with the club in Paris."

We sat down with our drinks in front of us.

"I think I'll go home and relieve the babysitter and get Ginny and a little bag and then we'll come back. But don't wait for us. I'm used to sleeping in your daddy's bed and she sleeps so well in her little bed in the room in the back. And she loves it when you're home and you can tell your stories and listen to hers. Maybe she can take your mind off things."

Something on my face prompted a second bad idea.

"Or, we can pull out Ginny's trundle bed," she said. "I could sleep with her. It don't make me no never mind. But I don't think you should be by yourself. And only for tonight. I'm going to Chicago tomorrow where I'll be presenting at the Black Business Women's Expo."

"Neither one."

She got up and threw back the last of her drink. "You know, I am kind of your stepmother. You don't have too many other people to talk to. Am I right?"

Neither one of us expected me to answer. But, as I stood up, I felt the need to tell her, "You know, although my father cared for you, and he loved Virginia, he didn't bring you into my life as my stepmother."

She didn't miss a beat. "I've got one for you. Did you know Obsidian has a serious girlfriend? I think he's going to marry her. And I'm going to need a key."

She tossed her head, and I let her walk upstairs and out the door before I followed and locked it behind her. I had forgotten what a bitch she was. But remembering to be mad at her was a welcome distraction during a restless night.

CHAPTER · 19

The alarm went off at six o'clock on Thursday, and the next sound that landed was the rain. It took a minute before I could manage to sit up, and my mind was storming while I dialed the patient information number at Harlem Hospital.

"Critical but stable."

The same. Like last night. The nurse who answered the phone on Obie's floor found my name on some list and told me he was asleep.

I ignored the blinking message lights—lots of them—and sat down on the cushion in front of the window. November had taken the leaves off the ailanthus tree branches so they were no longer blocking the light or blocking my view of the tops of the stately Stanford White-designed yellow brick houses across the street, some with terra cotta detail.

The first bell on my meditation timer landed in my chest and the last three bells landed in my belly. In between, I was aware of my body breathing.

I sat a minute longer and allowed the sadness to drop out of my mind where it was a story and into my heart where I felt it with some tenderness. I took another breath. Letting go.

The first two blinking phone messages were from friends I shared with Cecelia. But I decided I didn't want to make our sad connection yet, and, instead, I got up and started taming my personal space.

Since anywhere I live resembles the inside of my head, the act of making the bed was the act of going sane.

I took a bath in the big claw-foot tub and left the bathroom clean and the window open to the cool wet air. And I dressed quickly, pulling my hair behind my neck, putting on flat shoes and the pants to one of my business suits. But I left the fitted jacket in the closet and chose a roomier one. Then I turned at the mirror to make sure it was as loose as I needed it to be.

I sat down at my mother's vanity in front of a small tray of shiny things I had hidden from the women who descended in those desolate days when she was first dead, and the perfume bottles and her teacup. The little black funeral hat with the veil was perched on the top edge of the mirror.

One of the pictures caught her at an age I had long since passed with her husband and her new fat baby. She wore a flower in her hair. In another, my father was a boy, standing with his rifle and a dead doe and his proud father in a Kentucky woods.

By the time I took the stairs, the upstairs space and I were both at least presentable.

My father's floor was still piled with newspapers and magazines and precarious towers of books. The hat rack displayed kangols and baseball caps and cowboy hats. I was going to ask the men who cared for him to come and help me tackle his space when I got back to town. Perhaps they might answer the questions I didn't get a chance to ask him.

The parlor floor looked like I left it the night before—the antiques and finds restored and upholstered by Scotty, the piano, the sideboard, the African art and the gun rack.

That's important. I needed to find my stuff where I put it. For one thing, sometimes I heard sounds and thought some ax murderer or some vampire was in the house with me. And even on a good day, it annoyed me to find the messy remains of anybody else in my space, even if it was some friend or some lover. Being lonely when it's late is the small and occasional price I pay for having my spaces to myself.

Actually, if the truth be told, the price of the space I was going to buy in California was neither small nor occasional. It would take every nickel of the money I'd already made for *Last Stop, Harlem*, which enough people saw to do me some good.

I unlocked and stood in front of the gun rack and picked up the .380 that I practiced with the most because my father said it would best fit in my handbag. It would, but I was thinking I'd carry it in the holster under my jacket.

Whoa. And do what?

It was a personality I could put in the space where safety needed to be. Safety had felt like Daddy and Obsidian, each of them, and both of them even at a distance, now neither of them. Facing the truth as it appeared in that moment gave me pause to think.

Okay. Was I really going to shoot somebody? Lt. Knight wasn't even real. But neither was I, actually. It gave me a minute to consider that the permit for the gun wasn't a carry permit, besides being expired. And then there was the matter of my primary residence being California. I put the holster and gun back.

I went to the kitchen and sat down with my coffee and a legal pad and one of the good pens. The way my memory works is it takes a picture. I retrieved from my memory some of what was stolen from the office the night before, including details I had lingered over but we didn't print.

What came to me were the names of the people and companies who made withdrawals. Not so many addresses. There was something troubling there, but I didn't focus. Too bad. I also sketched a grid of interlocking relationships to ask somebody about.

When I had gathered from my memory all I could, I emptied a red, black and green Harlem Week plastic tote to take with me so the newspapers I would pick up at Jocelyn's newsstand wouldn't get wet. And I put a small clutch in it rather than a big purse. It felt like I needed to be traveling light.

The phone rang before I could get out the door. It was Viola.

"I called the hospital. He's stable. Tell me how you feel," she asked.

"Like you would expect me to feel," I said, impatient with her tell-me-all-about-it tone.

"I want you to come by this morning for some breakfast," she said. "And Virginia wants to say goodbye in case she doesn't get to see you before you leave. I'm doing her hair. Don't make too much of Obsidian and Cecelia. I'm trying to keep from scaring her."

"I'm going to see Elizabeth Miller now. But I can be there if we call it brunch in probably two hours. I have some things I want to ask you."

"And I you. I'm going to Chicago, but I can catch a later flight."

CHAPTER · 20

There's something wonderful about a rainy day on a Harlem row house block.

The house on the corner was for sale. The one across the street was in the advanced stages of renovation, backed by a downtown bank.

We are aptly named Strivers Row, except our block is not land-marked like the houses one block north. I stopped at the bottom of the stairs at the Miller's house to look up at City College on the hill rising above St. Nicholas Park. Then I turned and walked up the stoop and used an ornate metal knocker to let Elizabeth Miller know I was there.

She was slightly overdressed for so early in the morning, in what I've heard described as good-walking-shoes. A brooch boasted an amber stone, the filigree repeated on her earrings. She wore an incongruous blossom of scarlet lipstick. But the makeup couldn't cover the puffiness.

After we held each other, she asked, "How are you? Marcus told me Obsidian was shot last night."

"The nurses tell me he's stable this morning. But I came to see about you. Can I help you do anything? Take something off your to-do list today?"

"Let's talk in the kitchen," she said.

Her kitchen was a modern contrast to the stained glass and antique ornamentation in the parlor, and it had been painted a deep eggplant.

"I have time for one cup of coffee. But we are going to need more time than that," she said.

"Yes," I agreed. "I woke up this morning and started to feel who I was going to be in my world, in my story, without Cecelia." I proceeded slowly, being careful of being clumsy with our shared grief. "Even though we were far apart, she was the best and dearest witness to my girlhood."

She smiled a little smile. "I heard some music. It brought her to my mind when you all were I think 5 or 6 years old and you were both twirling like banshees so fast and your mother and I could not stop laughing. And last night, I saw a young woman walking and something about her made my heart stop." Her voice caught but didn't break. "Thank you. I like talking about her. But is that why you came this morning?"

"I came for two reasons, to see how you are, and also, if I can, to ask you some newspaper questions," I said.

"It must be hard to sit in your father's chair at the newspaper. Have you discovered any tools you can share with me about how to handle your grief?"

"I have a meditation practice. I've made myself sit down and been surprised by moments of acceptance. But now we've lost Cecelia and I'm feeling our grief all fresh again."

"Yes. It is fresh and it is ours. Your father and I have been neighbors and friends forever."

We took a minute to regroup, before I asked, "I wonder if you know why Cecelia would give Mister Bell bank secrets. Did he tell you?"

Elizabeth Miller had been avoiding direct eye contact, as if her attention was on some internal conversation, but then she linked eye-to-eye with me. "Yes. The bank has been receiving warnings this year from the Comptroller of the Currency and she felt the board was taking advantage of its vulnerability rather than supporting the bank."

"Is that why she and Gary broke up?"

"She was calling attention to the bank's trouble to arouse the community and move the board to take action. Gary does not think it wise to tell bank secrets."

"I get that," I said. "Bank board business needs to be secret."

"There's more to it than that. He's playing for higher stakes than the souls of black folk now," she said. "That kind of access can change a person. His father would be ashamed of him."

"She gave some files to Mister Bell just before. I'm wondering if there's more."

Mrs. Miller went to the back door and took a heavy ring of keys from a hook. "These are Cecelia's extra set of keys. Some are the ones to the house and these are to I'm not sure what all. Come back whenever you can. I'm on my way out and I'll be out most of the day. Marcus wants to look around too. Maybe you two can look together when he gets here. He's going to come and stay with me." She smiled a small smile. "We haven't lived together since Cecelia was growing up and he came to be her daddy."

"I'll probably take a few minutes now and come back later when Mister Bell is here. Would it be okay?"

"Of course. I have a lot to take care of today." Her voice and attention trailed off.

I helped her gather her things and locked the door behind her.

I walked up the stairs to sit in my friend's space and to see what she might have been up to. On both sides of the staircase, paintings of musicians filled the walls in their separate frames. A framed front page of the *Harlem Journal* announced: HARLEM HISTORY REVEALED IN HOUSE TOUR. The Miller's house was featured.

What I could see of the second floor sitting room displayed an air of over-upholstered calm.

On the top floor, a tall long-legged metal bird peered a welcome at me and seemed to be looking over the bedroom from the corner next to the fireplace. Out the window I saw the top of our ailanthus tree.

Cecelia had been reading a book of poetry, three weekly magazines and a romance novel and writing in a stenographer's notebook that flipped from the top.

She was a woman who kept track of herself in a neat, tight, lefty script, and you didn't have to be a handwriting expert to notice when the writing turned personal and into a scrawl: *Damn. Damn. I do like a goodbye scene with words and pictures to chew on. Not these bits of sorrow and betrayal and the little nasty bits of greed.*

When she worked herself up, she even wrote an occasional poem.

I put the notebook in my plastic Harlem History Week tote.

CHAPTER · 21

There are people whose job it is to examine the dead, turn them over and turn out their pockets. That's what I did when I was playing a cop in the movies. A reporter's job is supposed to be a few steps removed.

Her closet looked like I would have imagined if had I stopped to think about the private side of Cecelia Miller all grown up. Her clothes were arranged neatly, dresses, slacks and skirts, blouses and jackets, each in their own territory. The shoes were mostly in their stacked boxes. I quickly opened the box tops and found only shoes, which was disappointing. That's a place where I would have stashed a secret. I stood on the vanity stool, sweeping the space between the top of the closet and the ceiling, and found only dust and not much of it.

I wondered how she could afford the oils and lithographs in the sitting room in the back. They were exquisite. An assortment of masks was sprinkled across one sitting room wall and a carved stool from Mali sat next to the Duncan Pfife sofa. Another large metal sculpture, this one of an angel, stood guard in another corner. In fact, my friend's space was filled with art and antiques.

I thought to myself, *all conditioned things arise and pass away.* I said out loud, "I love you, my sister."

I sat down and I tried to think of someone to call for comfort and new energy. It was way too early in California and I hadn't bothered with the New York crew in the three weeks since my father died, and now it would take too much to catch up. Then I smiled and called the floor nurse at Harlem Hospital.

"Baby! I needed you to call," Obie said."

He sounded like himself, only quieter.

"How are you?"

"Shot."

"Don't make jokes."

"Sorry. My shoulder needs repairing. But they're getting ready to do it. I could use a little company."

"I'm at Cecelia's. Can you have visitors later? Before the Apollo?"

"I can have anything I want. Why are you at Cecelia's?"

"To see if I can find anything else she might have tucked away."

"What have you found?"

"I just started. It's a little overwhelming."

"You grew up in one of those houses. Where did you hide things?"

I visualized it.

"Pearl?"

"Thank you, Obie. I'll call you back."

The cabinets in the dressing rooms of those houses are bird's-eye maple and there was nothing of interest in any of them. I pulled out each of the drawers under the marble sink and kept pulling, remembering when I was hiding my junior high school secrets. Nothing. But I kept pulling and sure enough, on the back of one drawer in the place where I used to hide the key to my diary was taped a key.

It didn't fit any of the drawers in Cecelia bedroom area. They were unlocked and I only tried them; I didn't look in. I felt like I was intruding, but kept at it. I also tried the drawers in her sitting room space. They were also unlocked.

But under the window was a wooden Chinese trunk, carved with the contours of a journey, and it was locked. The key fit and I lifted the lid.

Inside, a manila envelope was labeled with her left-hand scrawl, "September to November 1990." I pulled it out and found in it about a dozen sheets of paper.

The names of some of the companies inside were familiar. I found myself humming before I recognized many of the names included snatches of song titles or music makers: Louis Armstrong Associates, Handy & Son, Bottom Line Ltd., Satchmo & Co., Duke and Daughter, and simply Zing, Babylon and Louise. A dollar amount was written neatly next to each one. I love the imagination black people bring to our business, whatever our business is.

I put the envelope in my Black History Week bag.

Then I turned back to what was left.

Sitting at the bottom of the trunk was a Louise Vuitton speedy bag. When I lifted it, it was heavy and when I unzipped it, I discovered cash money neatly bundled in bank wrappers.

Twenty wrappers each bundled 100 dollar bills. I took out one bundle and counted bills at the corners. From the few I counted, I determined each bundle held 200 bills, for a pretty impressive $400,000. There were also bundles of twenties.

I realized I was holding my breath. This money was in Cecilia's trunk in the Miller's house. But it was not their money. How could it be? But it also was not mine. And now what? I couldn't very well put it back in the trunk and I couldn't very well put it back in the bank.

"Damn," I said out loud.

"Who is it?" somebody shouted from downstairs.

I closed the trunk and took the bag of cash with me to the wall connecting the top floor of my house to the Miller's house next door and opened the square of wainscoting on the wall. Ceel and I read that during prohibition, gangsters re-opened the space between two connected row houses to escape when the feds came in downstairs. It was the opening the builders had used to pass things back and forth when they were building the houses and then had closed up. When we tried opening the space in the party wall, the resulting disaster moved Daddy and Mrs. Miller to install a lintel beam and open a portal, which we used to our advantage over the years.

I put the stash of cash through the space in the wall against the large cabinet on the other side, closed the wainscoting, and went to see who was in the house.

CHAPTER · 22

It was Gary. And I met him at the bottom of the stairs.

"I was just leaving," I told him and walked past him. Then I turned back. "But let me ask you something." I took out my notebook and read his quote. "What is the truth behind the lies and innuendo surrounding Cecelia's relationship with the bank and with the people who love her."

"That's nobody's business," he said.

He walked to the kitchen and checked behind the door. "Shit."

Then he turned, "You were upstairs? What did you find upstairs?"

"You didn't answer me."

"You didn't answer me."

"I know this house from the time we were kids and we shared our spaces. I needed to sit with her things for a moment."

"You still didn't answer me. What did you find upstairs?"

I didn't consider for even a minute telling him about the money.

"I'm wondering what you think I would have found? Why would Mrs. Miller say your father would be ashamed of you?"

"She said that?"

"And she said you and Cecelia fought about what the bank board was not doing to save the bank."

"No comment."

He moved to stand between me and the stairs. "I hope you found whatever you were looking for because you are not going back upstairs. And I'm not leaving you here."

"I'm done for now. I'm on my way to pick up a copy of the newspaper. Have you seen it yet?"

"No. Why do I imagine I'm going to hate it?"

When I'm in New York, I always pick up a copy of the paper at Joselyn's newsstand at 135th and Malcolm X Boulevard, a couple of blocks over. I love the feeling of anticipation at seeing the *Harlem Journal* the way 200,000 readers in 60,000 households see it (or so they say, since the paper is not audited).

I watched Gary pick up the paper and skim the front page—stopping to read some of an article, but I couldn't be sure which one—then flip some pages.

He turned to me with the paper in his hand. "Your so-called revelations are wild and irresponsible, and you're affecting things you can't even imagine. Even the rendering of the Harlem movie theater. I don't know how you got it, but now every dog and his brother is going to try to get that project on his piece of dirt. They're already calling 110th Street SoHa, for South Harlem."

I snapped my fingers. "Morningside Heights wants to hook up with its dark uptown brothers?"

He didn't answer and walked away under his obnoxious umbrella.

"Good paper today, Pearl," Joslyn said. "Feels like you got yourself some ads too."

Blind Jocelyn passed along mostly what she heard about the edition from customers who bought theirs earlier in the morning. She no doubt could tell about the abundance of Veteran's Day ads from the paper's heft. It was nice and thick.

"Some people are talking about taking their money out the bank. Do you think I should take my money out?"

"Everything I know about the bank is in the newspaper," I told her. "Really. I have no idea. Except we don't want people withdrawing their money." I heard myself say "we." Interesting.

"Folks like the story 'bout poor Ceel," she said. "They say the paper looks like an advertisement for an action movie. And they like your publisher's letter and pictures of the vendors, the local lawless entrepreneurs, that's a good one."

"Thanks. I like it myself."

What you don't get without seeing it is the flair Al gave the paper. Once Daddy let him have his way with the layout, I have never been bored with the way the newspaper looks.

That's not always true about the way it reads and I flipped through to give the edition a spot check. Often, when my copy arrived in California, it would just lie in my hands like a dead thing full of camera-ready ads generated by liquor and cigarette manufacturers and stories sent by people with something to celebrate or an ax to grind. And then I would know they had missed. But this edition was alive. I put one copy in my tote.

I also put one each of the *Times*, the *Post*, the *News* and *Newsday* in one of Jocelyn's plastic bags, and I took the bag and my tote with Ceel's lists and notebook up the hill to Viola's in a gypsy cab.

CHAPTER · 23

Viola's house might have been the kind of showplace the Queen of Harlem would pull together for herself if she liked mock French provincial. There was even a small chandelier in the bathroom.

I was glad to have time to spend with Virginia before leaving again. Although I was home longer than usual, I had been so busy. She was now an eight-year-old dynamo with a face full of eyes and mouth and a head full of hair. Viola was on one side and I was on the other and we loosened the last few of the tiny braids while Ginny watched a video on a huge television.

"This is the kind of crap you're likely to buy on the street now," Viola said, indicating Ginny's murky movie and keeping her hands busy in the little girl's hair.

"Al is going to make some money with his first-rate copies," she said.

"You know about that?"

"Bobby scooped some of them up from the table yesterday morning," she said.

The video images were supposed to keep Virginia occupied while we talked woman talk. Somewhere in our distant girl memories we must have known her ears were tuned to our conversation; our words were all tangling in her crinkles like glitter. She was another black girl in a line of millions, hearing her version of what's real through the antennae on her regularly and roughly tended head.

I said as much to Viola who said, "Like boys in barbershops, only mostly all they hear is lies."

I asked, "The first thing I want you to tell me is why Daddy withdrew most of his money from First Amalgamated Bank?"

She stood up. Ginny said, "Ouch."

"Honey, let me finish making our brunch. Then we'll do the last of your hair."

Ginny starting singing, "Good-by. Good-by. Gotta go now."

"Do you know where that's from?" I asked her.

"Fingertips. Little Stevie Wonder. I can play 'I Wish' on my guitar."

"She loves *I Love Lucy* and The Temptations too," Viola said. "You know these kids are reincarnated from the boys from Vietnam. They brought their memories back with them."

We heard her singing up the stairs as I joined Viola in her kitchen where she was making chicken and waffles—one of her specialties—and flitting around in an apron. Daddy used to love that shit.

"I like the idea that maybe some boy or some girl might have returned as this beautiful, curious child," she said.

"I don't know what to think about past lives. But I do believe karma affects moment after moment in this life. For instance, you must be doing something right or something wrong really well. Your bar was all over Ceel's money lists."

"A bar is a cash business. You're liable to see a lot of activity from my bar at that bank."

"How long have you had your account?"

"My first husband had it when I got here and I kept it when he died."

"That's right. You came from Ohio."

"Ohio was where my ancestors came across from enslavement in Kentucky."

"You and Daddy had that in common. What made you leave and come to New York?"

"They counseled me to find my good elsewhere."

"Your ancestors speak to you?"

"Yours too. They all do. You all just don't listen."

"One more thing," I said. "I saw you with Bobby Bop on the street. How do you know him?"

"I'm a club. He plays at the Kat. It looked like he needed an intervention yesterday." She laughed. "It was fortunate for him that I decided to be on the street."

"I called you yesterday to ask you about it when I was writing the story."

"Pearl, I hope you're not going to keep investigating all this bank business and what happened to Cecelia. You seem to keep forgetting you're not a real cop. You've been out in Hollywood pretending to be a police woman. That's acting. That doesn't make this your job."

"I was ready to let Obsidian do it. But he can't now."

"Neither can you, Pearl. Get the glasses please. I'm making mimosas."

I went to the cherry cabinet with the stemware showing through glass. "House renovations? They must have cost you some money."

"They did."

"You all are doing quite well up here in Harlem. Cecelia has some lovely art pieces. Was she making that kind of money at the bank?"

Viola walked closer. "Pearl, I know you. You think you got where you are because you're smarter than any black person who lived before you showed up with Charles Washington as your daddy. But you need to let me know what you're doing. You really can't do this alone."

"Maybe," I said. And I made a decision that took me across the space I usually kept between her business and mine. "I found another withdrawal list Cecelia made. Can you tell me anything about these companies? They're not familiar to me."

I handed her the lists I had just taken from Cecelia's Chinese trunk and when she saw them she squealed, actually squealed. "I love this. You know some of these are music names. Let me make a copy."

"Why would she have a separate envelope with withdrawals from September until now?" I asked.

"I don't know. Did you find anything else?"

"What do you mean? Like what?"

"I don't know. Anything else?"

"Did you see the newspaper?" I asked. "Everything else is in the paper," I lied. And I handed her the copy of the *Journal* out of my tote.

"I haven't seen the paper yet. Let's sit down and I'll look it over while you talk to Virginia. I'm sure she has a story to tell. I love her stories. But, you know."

As I was leaving, she gave me back the original of the lists and I counted to make sure I had them all.

She held up the front page of the paper. "This front page is so real it's hard to look at. You took pictures of the car when he killed Ceel. But you don't have a photograph of the driver?"

"No. I was focused on her and he was driving away when I turned back to capture the car."

"I'll call you when I get back from Chi."

CHAPTER · 24

After brunch, it had stopped raining and I stepped across the street to the Kit Kat. Stevie was on the jukebox singing "Isn't She Lovely" and I didn't recognize the bartender. Deliverymen were moving things in and out. I ordered a Heineken.

"Vy's bartenders are all kind of special these days," I offered by way of conversation.

He didn't answer me. Reticence is a tricky thing in a bartender in front of a drinker who wants to talk. Then again, maybe he didn't have to be a talker with those defined muscles in his brown arms below the sleeves of his Rick James t-shirt.

He came back with my Heineken. "You're Pearl Washington the actress, aren't you?"

"Yes. And I'll call you Rick."

He had a killer smile on him.

I sat and watched him and the deliveries long enough to be in the way.

When I got outside, I decided to get the establishing shot of the stately sisters of connected sandstones that included the damaged building two doors away from Viola's house. It was still being secured and protected by tarps. But whoever was doing the work had left after erecting some scaffolding and posting danger signs.

I walked across the street and stepped around a police barrier and then stepped inside. It wasn't easy to navigate the site, but I took several pictures of the piece of brass with the house number that had shaken loose from the façade. The camera was as good as Karl promised and I could imagine a cluster of photos in a spread in the newspaper about this address where some of the fake companies on Ceel's list were supposed to be doing business.

Not wanting to broadcast my trespassing, I stopped before I stepped out, and I was careful to peek up and down the sidewalk. Then I flattened against the wooden support for cover and from there I watched Al, the newspaper's production manager, walking with Bobby Bop, the jazz man. As they reached the area where I was hiding, I held my breath until I heard their footsteps moving away. I saw them walk into the building next door.

Odd. Playing music at the Kit Kat Klub must have brought them together after the fight I witnessed out the window just before Cecelia was killed.

I walked around to the alley to get some pictures of the back of the stricken building. I noticed the back window was open in the building where Bobby and Al went in. Obie had identified the house as the site of the black-market factory which is probably why they needed the extra power of the generator that sat under a large 3-sided box. I left my bag with the newspapers beside the box, pulled over a milk crate and climbed up with my camera in my tote.

That's how I found myself standing, looking in the window at two rooms of a parlor floor apartment, which were stuffed with equipment and boxes. I recognized enough to figure out I was looking at audiocassette recorders and color photocopiers and the stuff you need to make hundreds of fake tapes at a time with fake packaging.

I thought the junk hid me because it kept me from seeing all the way into the front room. I took some pictures and was getting ready to climb down when the music stopped and I could hear their voices through the open window.

"I'm going to keep my two large to pay for what you stole yesterday off my table." I recognized Al's voice.

"We'll call that loan even," Bobby said. "But that includes the next movie. The deal is we'll buy your product and distribute it."

"I'm not doing a freelance business with you," Al said. "And that's not nearly enough money if I was. We're not talking about a tray of dance mixes or some crap shot in a movie theater with a camera in a backpack."

"Freelance is the only business you're going to do," Bobby said. "I don't have partners."

I took another picture of the scene, but then I had to include Al as he got bigger in the next shot when he covered the distance from the front to the back.

Al said, "Give me that camera."

"I don't think so," I told him.

He frowned. "This ain't no Hollywood movie, Pearl. You're going to get us killed."

"Got yourself a little problem?" Bobby Bop said as he walked from the front room.

"We've both got ourselves a little problem," Al told him. "This is Pearl Washington from the newspaper."

"Sounds like she needs to be persuaded to give up her camera."

When he got to us, I could see he had a 9 millimeter in his hand. Not good.

He was an understated crowd pleaser in a Zegna suit and a big gold Rolex watch. Although he'd probably never been called Red because he was a deep dark brown, there was red in his skin.

He got close and looked into my face. "I saw you in the movies. You look better in the movies. I almost hate to shoot you."

Al intervened. "You can't shoot her."

"Actually, I can," he said. "Give me the camera. And know you can't put any of this in your newspaper. You know that?"

I didn't know that, but it wasn't something to say. And I thought about what might buy me an exit from an impetuous action gone very bad. It was somewhat shameful to do it, but I decided to expose and therefore enlist the troops.

"This isn't a good place to make mischief," I said. "The movie police from L.A. have been watching this location and several others. You won't get away."

"I know about that. That's why there's no work happening and we have this space to ourselves today. But my people inside tell me we have a couple of weeks. We can get a lot done in two weeks."

Some noise might have warned me that the cops had arrived if I hadn't been so engrossed in the business on the other side of the window. Instead, the knocking at the street door downstairs made us all jump. It got louder, and then it turned into a battering sound that was not about permission.

The Hollywood P.I.s were breaking through the heavy reinforced front door downstairs.

Bobby ran toward the front. Al climbed out the window and we both climbed down from the wooden box. That's why the New York police people caught us on the ground in the alley.

"Put your hands in the air," was the first I heard from my police woman. I turned. She was probably in better shape than she seemed in the chunky bulletproof vest.

"I said put your hands up. Now!" she said to me.

That was a surprise. "Me?" I sounded shrill even to my own ears. Since when did the police make me nervous?

Al was not having a conversation with the New York City police-men who were pushing him toward the alley opening.

"You were maybe crawling into that window? Maybe you forgot your keys?" she said to me.

Sarcasm wasn't one of the things the sister was good at. But she was armed, so it probably didn't matter. The thing that disturbed me was that I couldn't tell whether she was serious about me being a suspect. I decided I'd better play it straight.

"I was eavesdropping on the conversation they were having in-side from the top of the generator outside. You saw me climbing down."

"We'll see about that."

CHAPTER · 25

I had to do the perp walk through a gauntlet of paparazzi at the 28th Precinct. I must say, I finally understood the impulse to put a coat over your head.

But my training and natural instincts kicked in, and I gave them a little smile, tossed my hair and squared my shoulders. Because I was posing, they caught me at it again and again. It didn't take long for someone to recognize me.

"Lt. Knight! Over here!"

"You've got something for him," one reporter said and shot his finger at me in Lt. Knight's trademark wisecrack. They all laughed.

"Thought you were a good guy."

I gave them the poster smile and would have stopped. But the police kept pushing me along, rather roughly actually. I suspect there's some resentment about cops who get a ridiculous salary and a happy ending. I left a message for Attorney Robinson who wasn't in the office when I called.

It appeared the big counterfeit movie bust happened while I was climbing on and off my spy box. The Hollywood militia were bragging about breaking a piracy ring in West and Central Harlem, Washington Heights and the South Bronx where they discovered duplicating machines and bootlegged copies of current hits, like

Godfather III, Ghost, Home Alone, Misery and last year's *Driving Miss Daisy* and *Last Stop Harlem.*

I wrote it all down.

It took a while to straighten things out, longer than it would have if the police had been willing to cut me some slack. The only message the detective who questioned me conveyed to me directly was that he was in charge and I was in trouble. Too bad it wasn't my friend Officer Stanley. At least we wouldn't have had to go through all the preliminaries.

He said, "Miss Washington, I'm tempted to lock you up just to teach you that you don't have a role here."

"Don't you worry. The only role I'm playing is journalist. Being arrested was an accident—yours and mine."

I didn't tell them about Bobby Bop. It felt like information I might be able to use. Maybe for a newspaper story when I got back. And I didn't leave the police station because I wanted to see about Al and because of my fascination with characters, probably the fascination that I turned into being an actor.

Thank goodness I didn't have the gun.

They gave me back the little pocket camera, and I didn't use it to take a picture of somebody's grandmother named Pinkie and her daughter being booked for selling drugs. But I did shoot the confiscated movie loot and the crowd of camera people.

That's why I was there when Adrianne showed up. They allowed her to go into the back and let me go with her.

Al stood up and shouted at me. "Did you have anything to do with them being there. Did you bring them?"

"Hardly. I had no idea. I'm just finding out about this business of yours."

"Your employers should be able to help get you out of here," Adrianne told him.

"I'm waiting for Reverend Garrison," Al said. "I called his office and they said he was coming."

"Why don't you leave word you'll be at the newspaper office?" I asked. "We'll see if we can speed things up."

"I prefer to wait for the reverend."

"He's a busy man. It may take a while."

"He said he was coming," Al said.

"First, how do you feel?" Adrianne said before I could continue arguing with him. "Then tell me what they've been asking you. It will give me an idea of the direction the investigation is taking."

I trusted Adrianne to get what Al was saying, while I let my mind chew on how my real life in New York was beginning to remind me of the make-believe I had left back in California.

They suddenly glanced over at me, pulling me back.

"It's hard for them to believe that people can change," Adrianne said.

I wouldn't have thought they had enough in common to be so intimate. She was gentle with him, and he was talking a lot but low enough to keep what he was saying between them. I felt left out, and I left them to it.

When Adrianne joined me in front she said she was going to wait, in case the reverend didn't make it.

"You care about him," I prodded.

"I just want to make sure they don't traumatize him. They're used to him being an addict. He's not anymore."

I decided to wait with her, and we were still there when the reverend arrived. He came in bellowing: "Where is he? Why won't you allow these men their recovery?"

You wouldn't guess he had an explosion like that in him. It happened when he started preaching too, all power and perfect pitch.

A young policeman stood up to confront the reverend and to block his entrance into the back. "You'll have to wait to talk to Carter."

The sergeant intervened and put his hand on the cop's shoulder. "Al Carter's in the back, Reverend Garrison," the sergeant said. "Maybe he can tell you why he can't stay out of trouble."

"Maybe you can tell me why you target the men in this community."

"Target is not the right word. Try keep an eye on or even attend to. That's how we do our jobs. Keeps you all safe and keeps us alive."

"The reverend is doing the Lord's work today," Adrianne said as we watched him fussing at the police."

"Is it the Lord's work that has him taking the coins out of his Harlem bank that are meant for redeveloping and growing the community?"

"Gary and the rest of the board are not the enemy."

"But he's not a hero."

She looked at me. "Yes. He is. Yes, they are. They're not perfect. But they're taking care of business."

"TCB," I said. "But without respect." Feeling a little proud of myself for making the Aretha Franklin reference, I slipped away without answering any more questions about Lt. Knight, action figure.

A shaft of sun emerged through the rain clouds. It was startlingly. I wondered why police stations in New York don't have windows?

Is it because they're afraid people will jump out? Or are they the fortresses they appear to be, built with civil insurrection in mind? I turned around to look again and discovered the whole top of the wall was filled with windows. Weird. It had felt so dark.

CHAPTER · 26

When I hit the lobby, one of the day guards ran up to me, like he'd been waiting.

"What are you hearing about Captain Bailey?"

"He's stable," I said. The standard routine.

He rolled his eyes. "What was that asshole after?" He asked. "You keep money up there?"

"Not money."

As I started to walk away, I thought to tell him, "Send someone up later. I want to change the locks."

"I was thinking it looks like he got in here with a key. And he ran out the back and got away right under the noses of the cops. They've been here all morning. Embarrassing if you ask me. Max too. He said he must have been upstairs when the punk got in and then somehow missed him when he made his rounds."

"Must have."

"And let me know if there's anything else," he said.

If you could banish the image of Obsidian bleeding on the floor, I thought, *that would do it for now.* But I didn't let the guard know that I needed more than he could deliver. There was no point.

"They've been calling from the bank," Adrianne said in the way of a greeting when I got upstairs.

She handed me a cup of coffee and a pile of notes. 'Irate' she had scrawled across the top of the bank president's messages. He had called early.

Reverend Garrison had also called some time before I saw him at the precinct. I tried to imagine him running down the back stairs late at night with the incriminating bank folder in his hands.

Calls from some other board members and the head of a Harlem-based state agency were also noted.

"Samantha took these before she left. She's at the precinct," Adrianne said.

"Why?"

"They're talking to everyone with keys. The locks on the doors weren't forced."

"You have keys."

"I have to go once you get settled," she said. "And I called a temp."

"You gave the police the list of people with keys?" I asked her.

"Of course."

"Give me that list. And anything you have that will help me make sense of this. Could you tell if anything else was missing from the safe?"

"Pearl, I think we should let the police do the investigating."

"Maybe," I said. "Maybe if Captain Obsidian Bailey was on the case."

There was no reason to let Adrianne, a key holder, know what was on my mind. And I didn't consider, even for a minute, telling her about the money.

"Thank you for the coffee Adrianne. And for being here this morning. We can trade lists. I found these withdrawals at Cecelia's just now. See if you ever heard of the companies on the list. And check the addresses. I noticed at least one is supposed to be located at the empty building that went down last night."

She read and said, "Very Harlem. Very cool. Very odd."

We walked back to the production room where the tables were moved away from the windows and where police tape stretched across the area near the door. Although no one was there, whoever had been there wasn't finished.

"I think Sam cleaned up the part they would let her clean this morning," Adrianne said. "Max said you had to be disarmed. I didn't know you could shoot a Luger."

I forced myself to look into her face and away from the distraction of the doorway and the memory.

"I practiced with my father since I was a little girl. I would have shot the sucker with Obsidian's gun if he didn't escape out the emergency door."

"Let me know if you need anything," she said.

"Like we talked about, I need you to do this job until I get back," I said. "And to tell me what's happening. I'm sure I'll hear plenty from the board. They want to take over. But I'm going to trust you to do what needs to be done in this interim period."

"I'm ready," she said.

"It seems so," I said. "I'm going to take the risk. I have been impressed with you over the couple of weeks, actually. We will be in constant contact. And I'll be back very soon."

In the general clutter and mustiness of the production room, Al's territory was stark and modern. Inside a big empty frame on the wall he had pinned odd landscapes, magazine ads and sketches, including the fantasy office and entertainment towers proposed for the empty lots. I recognized some of them. It would be nice to shop and see movies in places like that if they ever actually got built. Fat chance.

His desk was a slab of butcher block set on file cabinets. It was neat on top.

The temp showed up and she seemed genuinely pleased with herself to have landed a position at the *Journal.*

"Miss Washington, I'm Lois. Happy to meet you. I see Reverend Doctor William Garrison himself called."

"Pleased to meet you too Lois. I just talked to the right reverend."

"Really? He's my pastor," she said, all giddy.

She took a breath. "I heard you all were robbed. Do you think it's safe here?" She was tiny and neat and probably not as timid as she seemed.

Still, I was glad to reassure her. "There will be police officers around today. And remember to keep the door locked and to use the intercom. But I don't expect any trouble."

"I'll introduce you to the people working in the other offices," Adrianne said. "You can call them if you feel afraid."

As I walked away, I heard, "Oh, Miss Washington!" The temp was a little too exuberant for my taste. "The pastor had left his office when I called him back," she said.

"Don't return any other messages until I tell you to."

I went into the publisher's office to call California.

"Hi love," Roger said. "I saw you getting arrested just now in a raid on what they're calling a black-market video factory. Hands behind your back. The whole thing. Very sexy."

"It's a national story? Good."

"Lt. Summer Knight involved in a bust in Harlem. Great publicity. How'd you manage that?"

"Everything is connected. In fact, I've got a job for you. The newspaper's production manager is selling movies on the street. I took some pictures. Can you check to see where the post-production work was done? He said they were made from masters and haven't been released yet. Someone out there must be slipping him copies."

"Sure. I can do that."

"When we got busted just now, I was listening to him talking about selling hundreds of copies of some of those movie masters. It's also part of a story I'm interested in about the street vendors."

"I thought you were keeping your distance."

"My friend died in a hit-and-run murder. And Obsidian's in the hospital."

"Obsidian? The old boyfriend?"

"Yes. He was shot last night."

"I'm sorry, Pearl."

"Thank you. And also, Roger, tell my California meditators I'm going to lead a meditation class at the 28th Precinct in Harlem. And remember the merits of our practice benefit all beings. Of course, also tell them to be still and breathe."

"We've been doing a lot of walking meditation. I think they miss you."

When I hung up, I called Harlem Hospital but Obie was asleep.

CHAPTER · 27

When I got home, I called Mister Bell.

"I want to talk to you. Are you going to the Stop the Violence concert?" I asked.

"Liz and I were supposed to go. But maybe I will. I'm going a little crazy and she has her friends to look after her. Meet me at the bookstore. I want to talk to you too. Then we can walk over together."

I went upstairs and repositioned the fancy money bag where it landed when I passed it through the opening in Ceel's adjoining wall and where it was concealed behind the cabinet on my top floor. It was safe there until I could figure out what to do with it.

To get dressed for my date with Mister Bell, I found in the closet one of the outfits from the old days—an evening suit that I wouldn't be able to move in easily. It felt like I wouldn't need to move much just to hear some music. I felt exposed somehow in the little skirt and I felt a chill when I remembered Bobby Bop and his gun.

But, since I had no plans to be rummaging around in any of Harlem's houses or alleys in the few days I had left, I decided again not to arm myself. Instead, I picked up the small beaded evening bag that wouldn't have held a gun if I had a permit to carry one.

I took a car to the bookstore in the drizzle. Mister Bell was debonair, in deep blue velvet with a white shirt and a Kente cloth tie and cummerbund.

"You look marvelous," I said.

"As do you," he said. "We can talk in the back."

We left the young woman at the cash register and the readers and browsers and shoppers to their stories.

Books and newspapers and flyers were balanced precariously in piles on all the surfaces, including the chairs. But Mister Bell had obviously done this before and he set one stack on the floor to make room for me. The Broadway playbills and issues that concerned him were taped all over the walls.

He sat in his overstuffed chair with more books as backdrop.

"I'm only here because I trust you. Am I wrong?" I asked.

"You can trust me," he said.

"I found some cash at Cecelia's. And I was wondering how does somebody get big chunks of cash like that any way but stealing it. I wouldn't have expected that of her."

"I wouldn't either. What did you do with it?"

"It's in a safe place for now."

He leaned toward me. "This is important. I need you to tell me what you're doing. I don't want you to get hurt. Don't go freelancing on me. I need to know how this is unraveling. Can you do that?"

"I can let you know what I'm doing. But Daddy used to say I have talk face. People love to tell me stories. And I have Charles Washington connections. I can do this."

"But you need people. We all do. I know I always need my posse to cover my back."

"I envy you. It feels like I'm losing the few people I have. Obsidian and Ceel were both my people."

"Yes. But Obsidian is still alive. And you and Ceel will always be connected. I remember when you were girls. You were funny little people. Busy with your plans. Daring each other to do the scary things."

He stood and waited to give me a hand to get up.

"I'm not finished with this conversation, this remembering. But let's go hear some music. We deserve it."

⸻◆⸻

When we got to the Apollo, we watched Adrianne, a showstopper in a purple pants suit, walk into the elevator with Reverend Garrison, while we were stuck waiting in line in front of a tiny woman all in black, including lipstick. The bit of brown-skinned beauty blocked the elevators with attitude and with an ominous male, also in black, who stood behind her.

The sister was having none of a small group who swore they were invited guests. She said something to her partner who went to check out their story and, after she had banished them to a corner away from the roped entrance, she turned her attention to us.

"Yes?" It was just the right suspicious touch.

"Marcus Garvey Bell, Freedom Bookstore, and Pearl Washington, publisher of the *Harlem Journal.*"

"You should stand at the side there while we check the list," she said and I, who have stood before the Hollywood best of them, thought I had never felt so dismissed.

When we got upstairs to join the inner circle, Mister Bell and I separated to mingle. I didn't see him again until I joined him standing in the aisle between our well-worn seats in the beautiful theater.

He waved his arm at the stage. "I used to stage manage here," he said. "I remember once we had a blackout during a Gloria Lynn concert and put on the show with flashlights and candles. It was beautiful."

I hugged him. "Thank you. I love those stories about the old days. I'm going to get a drink before the show starts. Can I get you something?"

He looked at me without smiling. "The old days? That is not all the information I have that you're going to need. And no, I don't need anything to enjoy this music."

The first set started sweet and smooth and when Bobby came on we were more than spectators, moving as he played us. And we only let his group go when the stage hands and tech started setting up for the headliner. The anticipation was palpable and full of the energy and the magic of the haunted space. And it was crowded with James Brown and Dinah Washington and Billy Holliday and the kids who won Amateur Night and the ones who lost, and it was sacred. I remembered being there as a little girl with my father. I finally released for those hours and let it all go.

I was getting my one-for-the-road just before they closed the bar at the end of the show, when Adrianne walked up.

"Al was supposed to be the stage manager tonight. But he's still on the rock," she said. "They let him call his job and he got word to me that he wants me to go to his crib to see how 'the company staying at his house is doing' is how he put it. I figure it's to see about Heavy."

"Why?"

"Al's clean. Your father hired him when got back from rehab and he's excited about his life. He's afraid Heavy is using and bringing dope into his house. I don't want to go alone. Will you go with me?"

"I'll come."

"Hurry."

"Are you sure?" Mister Bell asked when I told him I needed to take care of some newspaper business, and he didn't have to go with me.

"Maybe I'll get back in time to hear some of the rest of the music."

He looked annoyed and relieved.

CHAPTER · 28

Al lived in the apartment on the ground floor of a brick and brownstone row house on 136th Street between Seventh and Eighth Avenues. Adrianne and I had to maneuver over the stones inlaid in front that were slick from the earlier rain. A fish tank was visible through one window. I hit the knocker and rang the bell and called out and heard something, but no answering welcome. Adrianne moved a paving stone and found the key. I stood in the recessed entryway under the parlor floor stairs and rang the bell again and then leaned against the filigreed wrought iron gate to hear what I could hear.

I had to move out of the way so she could unlock it and we peeked in together and stood near the door, waiting to give Heavy time to get his business straight. I expected him to come out of the bedroom half-dressed. Young men, it would seem to me, would have need of a little privacy.

The wall in front of us was full of color above a mess of spray cans. It took a minute to find Heavy's name under the painted crowd.

"It looks like he tagged Al's wall," Adrianne said.

"It's complicated. And it makes me sad," I said. "But I like it."

A drum set sat in the middle of the floor, probably ready to go back in front of Heavy's wall art.

An industrial-strength metal rack held an audio system in six parts, several videotape recorders, two monitors and shelves of tapes. Al's movie and music business must have been good for him to be able to afford the stuff. I knew what he made on his day job.

Two long Chinese swords stood in an umbrella stand next to the shelf which also held other Japanese weapons, including nun chucks and a throwing star.

On the other side of the room, a large canvas hung from one of its corners. A mess of coffee cans and brushes and hand tools filled one milk crate and two others were full of armatures to build sculptures on. A stone seemed to be standing upright on a rolling pedestal with some shaping that looked like movement; although it did not yet have a form.

"I told you Al was making art again since he came back from the drug rehab," Adrianne said. "Look at this place."

She walked over to the studio side of the room and bent down to gather some of the loose bills scattered on the floor. She turned to show me.

I called out, "Heavy?" And I crept down the hall past the little kitchen and the bathroom.

By the time I got to the bedroom, curiosity had beat out any bit of leftover embarrassment. I was hurrying, wondering what I would find next. Nosey and I busted through the door to find a man lying on the floor by the bed.

"Adrianne, come here quick!"

He was lying on his side in a blue velour Reebok tracksuit. I knelt to feel for the pulse in his neck. His body was warm and I could move his arm, but the blood wasn't flowing. His heart had stopped pumping.

His bare feet were dirty but well kept. Fit and young, he should have put up a fight. But there he was, just lying there like he was sleeping with an open eye staring out at nothing now that whoever it was he looked at last was gone.

A baseball bat was lying next to him with something on it I didn't want to look at too closely.

I knew the routine, and without moving him, I saw the open wound in his head and the bruises and the cuts and swelling around his mouth. His lips looked like they would have healed crooked.

I felt Adrianne kneeling beside me.

"It's Heavy, isn't it?" I pitched my voice low and respectful.

"Yes. Is he dead?" she asked.

"Yes."

"How do you know?" She touched his hands, felt for his pulse, and touched his neck. "Oh shit."

Then she said what it meant to her: "Not now. He . . ." Her voice cracked.

"These are old bruises. I saw them last night when he was arrested on the street in front of the Kit Kat. And what happened tonight maybe didn't hurt him because he was very high." I pointed to two tiny empty clear plastic vials and one colored top. "What a waste. What a stupid horrible waste."

I got on my knees and found the phone under the quilt on the floor. From there I could also see under the king-sized bed. My view was not obstructed by anything except a precious few very small tufts of dust and Heavy's sneakers where he must have kicked them off. And I saw Adrianne's hands reaching down to pick up one of the empty vials. I looked up to watch her walk over to open the back door on the garden. She stood there looking out.

When I picked up the phone there was no connection. I put the phone back on the floor and went to stand beside her.

"Are you going to be all right?" I asked. She didn't answer.

I turned around, and it occurred to me I had heard some noise when we rang the bell. "Do you think somebody could still be in the apartment?" I asked her.

I walked over to the closet and threw open the door. Nothing. We both reacted with nervous noise that was not laughter.

"Adrianne? Don't touch anything else. Can you give me a minute? I want to share something with Heavy. It's a chant to Quan Yin, who hears the cries of the world. It's something to carry him with compassion."

Adrianne said, "I want to sit with his art." And she went back to the front.

I chanted. Then, I went to stand in the back door where the smell of dirt was a rich mix, not yet frozen and kind of wonderful in New York City. I could still smell the rain.

When I switched on the floodlight, it reached just beyond the pile of flagstone pavers near the door and illuminated part of the incongruous fairyland of Al's tranquil garden space of empty branches and evergreens and a stone bench beside a silent fountain.

He hadn't finished paving the dirt path and I saw sneaker prints made by a kid, or a little grown person, running and sliding to where it was dark but where there wasn't any place to hide.

The large wooden box at the fence sent back the smell of compost in the humid air. The floodlight caught the night above the top of the fence.

Back in Al's bedroom, I stepped over the doorsill and felt a chill at the back of my neck as I looked down at the floor at Heavy, still dead.

I called out, "Adrianne!" The silence got louder. "Adrianne!"

She didn't answer.

"Adrianne, is that you?" She still didn't answer, which meant it probably wasn't her walking at the front of the house.

I tipped over to the door and got outside and flipped off the floodlight and took off my shoes and ran in the dark, avoiding as best I could the path with the sneaker prints.

At the back fence, I had to stash my beautiful black stilettos on top of the compost box to free my hands, and I had to hike the little skirt to my evening suit further up my thighs to free my legs for the climb on the step stool next to the compost box. Since I couldn't see over the fence, I couldn't tell if there was another backyard adjoining Al's yard on the other side where I would be trapped once I went over. But climbing the wall was my only option.

I got as far as the top of the box and I was commending myself when the floodlight went up and I heard a voice call out, "Stop! I suggest you come back here."

CHAPTER · 29

I had the nerve to be mad, until I turned around and got a look at the silhouette of a man standing center stage with the light behind him. Even from there I could see his handgun reflecting the light and looking comfortable in his hand. It convinced me to abandon my attempt at escape over the fence, which probably would have been tricky anyway in the stupid skirt.

I turned to get my shoes off the box.

"Stop! Now! Put your hands up and come back here."

I walked again along the edge of the path in my stocking feet, avoiding the footprints. But he messed up the prints when he covered the last distance separating us and reached out to grab my arm. Then he dropped his hand.

It was Bobby Bop. "This is close enough," he said. "You can't get anywhere I can't reach with this." And he gestured toward the fence with his gun. "Maybe we'll go see what's in the box."

"Oh please. Not the mud again."

"Move."

We walked to the compost box and he stood on the step stool and tossed me my shoes. I considered running, but he was right that there was nowhere to go the gun couldn't reach.

He opened the lid and damn if he didn't find something. "Aha."

He used a stick to dig around some more in the box. When he

didn't find any more of what he was looking for, he hefted out a small suitcase. It looked dry but it had little wheels and the wheels were muddy.

"I liked the show tonight," I said. "It was just what I needed." He didn't answer.

"How did you get away when the movie police busted us this morning?"

He still didn't answer. But I kept talking while we walked because it lightened the death-march aspect of our return trip through the garden. The wheels got muddier as he rolled the suitcase back.

"Why are you here? Is that money? I overheard you and Al talking about making bootleg movies. Was he really making suitcases full of money? And how did you know?"

We were at the door and we looked down at Heavy while time stopped.

"He was a little wannabe hustler. Wasn't going to have much else happen to him than this anyway," he said.

"Then why kill him?" I asked. It was a question to maybe start a conversation now that he was talking back, while I paid attention to the space I had to maneuver in. There was no way I was getting enough room to use the baseball bat, even if I could have made myself touch it.

He wiped some of the mud off his Sly Stone concert boots on the carpet before he shoved me from behind down the hall. When we got to the bathroom, I reached in and grabbed one of Al's thick towels. He waited while I wiped off the mud. I would have been taller than him in the heels but I didn't put the shoes back on.

When we got to the living room, he opened the suitcase. In it was money in batches wrapped with rubber bands nestled in bunches of loose bills.

"Look at that," I said for lack of anything better to say.

He closed the lid and rolled it to the door.

"Is that why you killed him?"

"I didn't kill him. I want people alive to pay me."

"You're the loan shark. That was the loan you were talking to Al about."

"I'm a businessman."

"I thought you were a music man."

"It doesn't pay the bills."

"Do you know who killed Heavy?" I asked.

"He got paid to scare Cecelia and he killed her with the cab. Bunch of idiot niggers."

I didn't expect him to tell me. It was probably not a good thing. But if he was talking, I needed to know.

"Why? Why would somebody try to scare Cecelia?"

"To make her shut up."

"About what?" I asked. "About the bank?"

"Your newspaper let everybody know the bank wasn't safe."

"Aren't you curious to see how much is in the suitcase?"

He stopped for a moment. "There will be time."

He turned to the business of searching Al's inventory and picked up one of the videotapes. I was thinking about my options and they seemed like a precious few. I moved close enough to the rack and to Al's throwing star sitting on one shelf. My teacher had given me a shuriken and instructions on how to use the eight-pointed star as part of my training.

"I buy product. That's good business. But I don't like negotiating at a disadvantage," he said.

"Is that why you killed Heavy? He was just at the wrong place? He was just in your way?"

"I've got a better story. Too bad you won't be writing it Pearl Washington from the newspaper. I know this town. I went up and over the house today to get away from the bust. I always have a way out. And here's one you'll love. Whoever killed Heavy killed you too. Obviously."

I watched him turn back to the tape library.

"I'm going to get a tissue out of my little bag." The emphasis on the size of my beaded evening bag seemed to work and he looked up and then went back to another row of tapes. It was the last one. He squatted and hunched over to get a good look.

While he was preoccupied, I slid the throwing star off the shelf and took it into my hand then closed my fist so only the points showed between my fingers. I held it against me behind my beaded bag. Sometimes an instinct takes over all the available space in my head. My instinct told me to walk over to the front door. But he had had the presence of mind to lock it.

I turned two locks with one hand and felt it give.

"Get away from the door!" He shouted and moved across the room fast and grabbed me. I turned to say something to distract him, something to continue the conversation we were having, and only managed to turn slightly away before he punched me in the face.

I rooted myself, stepped forward, and my body drove my backhand to deliver the metal points of the throwing star between the knuckles of my hand, not into the lethal place in his throat, but into his cheek.

He howled and held one hand to his face. I grabbed the limp wrist of the gun hand and used my knee to push him back. He stumbled and I watched the gun fly off down the little hall. He started for it. And I was out.

There was really nowhere to hide on the sidewalk. When you see what people do on the sidewalk, you're not that quick to hit it. I heard him coming. And, I flattened myself against the building behind the little bit of wall the Urban League had built to enclose their front stoop next door and waited. From there I could hear his footsteps running toward Seventh Avenue.

CHAPTER · 30

I gave Bobby a minute and then I stood up and ran the few steps to the corner where I could see him walking down Powell and rolling the small suitcase and with the bag of tapes in the other hand. He heaved them into his Caddy and drove away.

I heard the deep comfort of a bass voice. "Probably going to the Kat if I know Bop."

I whirled around to find two men I didn't recognize at first in the dark. One pushed a handkerchief into my hand. They were Daddy's friends Riley and Joseph. I put the handkerchief up to my nose.

"Better have your eye looked at. And you'll need to pack your nose," Riley said.

"Listen to Riley," Joseph said. "He knows about working in the corner on broken noses."

"Soon as you call the police. Somebody killed Heavy and the phone is dead in there too."

"Clarence is dead in there?"

"He's dead in there."

"Damn."

"How long have you been out here?" I asked them.

"We stopped for a minute before we went to Ruthies to watch the Brooklyn Nets play some basketball. We saw Clarence go in. He had a bag."

"And when we came back and saw the gate open, we decided to wait and see what was going on and that's when we saw you and Bobby running out."

"Did that son of a bitch do that?" Riley asked.

"Yes. Bobby Bop punched me in the face."

Riley went to find a phone, and Joseph and I walked over to Al's.

While Joseph went down the hall to verify Heavy was dead, I wrote down what I remembered from the reels and videocassettes that were gone and a description of both Bobby Bop and what I remembered of Heavy and how he was lying—just to have them.

"Heavy changed his clothes," Joseph said, when he came back from the bedroom. "He must have a whole wardrobe of those suits. Maybe they were in the bag he brought in."

"Or, it might have been a bag of money. Bobby found a suitcase of money hidden in the back in the compost box."

"Maybe. But he always wears a sweat suit with a hood. But red. The sweats he was wearing was red."

"Don't tell the police the thing I said about the money. Okay?"

We told the police everything else. They kept us in the living room in one area near the door and took samples from our hands and clothes. I heard Heavy's injury described as traumatic head injury and the drug inventory to include marijuana, crack, Valium and fentanyl.

While detectives were making field tests and taking pictures, Riley ministered to my face.

When I was sitting across from the detective, he picked up a plastic bag with the throwing star in it and turned it over several times and touched his thumb against one of the 8 points. "Is this blood?"

"No comment."

"You know I could get you for criminal possession of a weapon in the fourth degree for this. It's a class A misdemeanor to carry that thing around."

"It's not mine."

He asked me again to describe the crime scene, now very much changed, compromised, he called it. He seemed surprised when I described it the same way as last time.

"How do you know what's missing? You said this was the first time you were here."

"I didn't say I know everything that's missing. I just know Bobby took some of the cans and videotapes with him."

I didn't tell him about the money—not the loose bills Adrianne picked up off the floor or the suitcase of money in the compost box.

"Miss Washington, you should buy a lottery ticket," he told me. "You're lucky he let you get away."

"I don't know. Seems to me I've used up a lot of my luck. But not tonight. He didn't *let me* anything."

When we walked outside, we got our pictures taken by the downtown news people.

At Harlem Hospital, they described the gauze packing Riley had inserted as a professional job and my nose as not broken.

At home, I slept iced and propped up with pillows.

CHAPTER · 31

By Friday morning I was feeling the effects of not having had a good night's sleep in a couple of days. And it felt like Bobby's fist broke through my protective layer of busyness and denial. And it was also Friday when some of the details came together. Looking back, I wonder how I missed it.

It was early, but I had already discovered that Elizabeth had gone out, and I wasn't getting any better at this death business. Daddy's seemed almost part of the natural order of things when compared to these latest losses. And I could only visualize Ceel dead. I had a whole gallery of living images of her laughing, busy, dancing. But now, I only had the vision of her lying on the street.

First, I called Viola and waited while I got a little Phyllis Hyman and a request to speak slowly and leave a detailed message with a time and a phone number. And the wish for a blessed day.

"Viola, I'm thinking I might want to see a plastic surgeon. When you get back from Chicago, let me know how to get in touch with your person." When I hung up, it occurred to me I'd never heard her say she had one, although she obviously did.

Then I called Adrianne. "Where'd you go? You left me with that mad man."

"You said you wanted to look around and I had no idea the murderer would come back. You told the police I was at Al's. I was up half the night dealing with their accusations. I suppose they wanted to see if our stories jived. And, by the way, they asked me again where I was the night before when Obsidian was shot since I have keys to the office."

She was indignant, and then not.

"But, girl, you are all over the news this morning. At the scene of a murder last night, and at the precinct being arrested, looking like a movie star. Are you okay? Is your nose broken or anything?"

"It's not broken but I need to have someone look at it. My fans won't like it if it turns into a bump or something. Do you know a plastic surgeon?"

"I do. But, you know, forgive me, but you can't pay for that kind of publicity."

"Except a young man died and I got punched in the face."

When I got outside, the morning remains of the day before spoke to the activities that had taken up the time of my neighbors. The leftovers from meals at the fish place had spilled or been dumped from garbage bags. What looked like someone's entire belongings were piled in front of the single-room occupancy hotel aptly named Stop Inn. And empty crack vials and their absurdly innocuous pastel tops studded the pavement on the next block.

Stores were doing a good business on Lenox Avenue in Harlem in 1990 and long stretches of them beckoned with the names of their owners: Majester's, Virginia's, Lucille's, Bernice's, Vernon's. Others lured more seductively: Welcome Restaurant, Friendly Vegetable Market, Community Grocery.

And then there was simply: Eats, Fruits and Liquor. Liquor had been open since the crack of 8 and the early birds were already heading back down the boulevard in ones or twos with their morning hits in hand.

I navigated through my neighbors who caught up with each other on corners and stoops.

The herds of cars and trucks stampeded at the pedestrians strolling across the crosswalk. Twice on the way, I gasped, once when one very old woman couldn't, and once for an adolescent who wouldn't, hurry to move out of the way. It's a wonder.

The several men who swept in front of the stores barely paused for pedestrians. But when they paused, they spoke: "Mornin."

"Morning to you too," I said.

At 125th Street in front of the fenced empty lot where the bazaar begins, the once and present Africans were setting up tables in their allotted reserved spaces.

"Good morning, my sister." A brother's smile stopped me.

"Do you have Universal Love?" I asked him, standing in front of his table full of incense and oils and brass and wooden things to burn them in.

"No. But I have musk, kickass, strawberry and pussy."

"Never mind." I put a tiny incense burner back on the table.

"Use this on your wrists and you'll have a bountiful day."

I barely dodged his out-stretched finger. Patchouli wafted after me.

Other business people were laying out bolts of fabric and hanging garments on the fence. Hats covered a table in color-matched piles and adorned Styrofoam heads on sticks clipped all around the table's edges. Dolls and dresses and carved wooden animals filled the next table. And tapes and beads and belts and jewelry were arranged in the prime spot just at the corner next to the IRT subway station.

It was a good time of morning before the demands of one of my long days kicked in.

"Braid your hair?"

The trio of Senegalese beauties took up more than half the sidewalk as they tried to stop people trying to walk by.

"No thank you," I said to the first one and only shook my head when the next two asked.

Before it got too crowded, the avenue could have been Tombstone. The hunks of hair that escaped out the doors blew down the boulevard like tumbleweed.

But now the day was starting.

Beyond the women, three tour buses were setting loose a crowd of white tourists in front of the Apollo to get their pictures taken. They would probably be Germans and Japanese, or out-of-towners from the Midwest. White New Yorkers usually didn't come uptown unless they worked in a state office, needed to renew their licenses, were headed for Metro North trains or were driving though on the way to the Triboro Bridge.

But I have to admit that I couldn't be sure because I didn't get close enough to hear them speak.

And the persistent part of the city that was Harlem had pulled me back for another day.

CHAPTER · 32

When I got to Harlem Hospital, they let me in to see Obie.

"He needs to sleep," the nurse said.

His skin contrasted dark against the pillow. His pajamas were a startling crème silk with a bit of blue trim. One pajama arm was draped over a bulge that would have been bandages and a sling.

I sat and took his other hand and breathed with him. And I watched him sleep. I did. That's a reason it's called a meditation practice. At that moment, I couldn't have started from scratch to figure out how to let the fear drop from my mind where it was a story to be embodied with a kind of tenderness. But I had a reference to touch the place where we were connected, no matter what. I breathed and watched him, and I watched my feelings change and settle and discharge. He told me later he felt me.

After I left him, I went about the business of a little fact-finding. Al was still in jail, but his landlady was impressed enough with my expired press pass and a Lt. Summer Knight autograph to let me look out into the backyard from her upstairs window.

Sure enough, there was a gap in the wall of buildings beyond the back fence where one had gone down and where whoever killed Heavy could have made his way over Al's fence and through the gap to 135th Street. Except, he would have had to brave the high branches and bushes against the opposite side and face the 32nd Precinct on the downtown side of the street. But he probably didn't look like a murderer and a robber and a drug dealer and whatever else, once he got over the fence.

And if it was Bobby, he even came back.

I walked across Seventh Avenue to Ruthie's. It was just as I remembered when Daddy used to take me there to eat chili and saltines. Mister Bell's friends were drinking coffee in their designated places, facing the door.

"Good morning," I said. "I came to thank you for looking out for me last night and to ask you again what it looked like at Al's place from across the street."

"Heavy showed up, like I told you, in his red sweat suit. Al must have let him in," Joseph said.

"Al was in jail."

"Then I don't know. When we came back after the Nets game we saw the gate open and we saw you and Bop running out," Riley said.

"Pearl, we were talking about last night. You know, Riley didn't call the police. He was looking for a working pay phone when he heard sirens."

"I wish whoever it was had made the call before he punched me."

"Your face looks like it's going to be fine."

"Thanks to you. They were impressed at Harlem Hospital with the job you did on my nose."

"He pulled back a little, I think. It could have been worse."

"Thank you for looking out for me. Do you know where Mister Bell could be?"

"He's taking this hard."

"The only thing I can think is that he's following a lead in the case."

"He's going to solve this thing."

"I hope he gets some help. It could be dangerous," I said.

"He has sense enough."

"And he knows he ain't no young man no more."

Their back-and-forth made me feel relieved and safe. My memory served up the two of them, two of the regulars my father stopped to argue and laugh with when I used to walk around Harlem learning who was friend and who was not by the touch of his feelings passing through our palms, with no censure.

"Please tell Mister Bell to call me if you see him before I do. And I'll come back later when he gets here," I said.

I put on my sunshades and took a matchbook with Ruthie's number on it.

⸺◆⸺

It occurred to me I needed to get additional information about the bank. I could do it just a few blocks over at the Arthur Schomburg Center for Research in Black Culture.

The bank files were massive and I decided they called for a laser light of specifics rather than the lamp of curiosity I was bringing to the search.

There was plenty about board members, including our Right Reverend Doctor William Garrison. I looked through some of the clippings from magazines and back issues of newspapers, including ours. There were stories about the church and about his community development organization—Harlem Village. I even got a clip about how much one of his houses was worth when it went on the market. There were pictures of Gary and Cecelia hobnobbing with national politicians and big-name movie and music stars. A magazine interview turned out to be slick and unremarkable. The reporter failed to penetrate his well-constructed facade. She pitched him softballs, which he hit easily with his talk of community and accountability. He's not a choirboy but nothing had ever stuck.

Protecting his reputation would be essential for maintaining his empire, and he looked like a man who had political aspirations—both strong motives for taking desperate action.

I also made notes for a feature about Mister Bell with the wonderful photos in his Schomburg file, most of which we also had in the *Journal* archives, including playing basketball for City College, fighting for community control of the schools, the bookstore. All of it.

Because I could, I looked up Captain Obsidian Bailey. One reporter called his 28th Precinct the most corrupt in the city because of the drugs, the most political in the city because of all the churches, and the most famous because of the Apollo. Sprinkled here and there, in addition to the action photos of Obsidian working, were the society pictures of the man about town with women on his arm. One woman looked somehow perfect beside him.

CHAPTER · 33

At 2:30, I was sitting at the bar at Showmans next to Reverend William Garrison, far enough back to make room for my legs and sideways so I could put my notebook on the bar. His stool was close enough to mine to smell Bergamot. Nancy Wilson was singing "Fly Me to the Moon."

He ordered a Dewar's splash. I ordered a vodka martini and a little straw to finesse the drink around my swollen lip.

"Your face looks like it hurts."

"It does."

The bartender checked behind the bar but it was too early in the cycle for any articles or pictures from the free-lancers who dropped their stuff at Showmans when the newspaper office was closed.

"Tell you what," he said. "See if you can convince the board not to take legal action to stop you."

I flipped to the page in my notebook and read some account names to him. "The owners of these accounts all but closed them. It looks like Cecelia was not killed on purpose. It was supposed to be a warning. So, it's not a murderer we're looking for. It's someone with a secret. That's you and your board. And one or more of these."

"I'll tell you one thing. The only way you can take this bank story on is if you're ready to leave town and never come back."

"That sounds like a threat." I wrote down what he said word for word. "And I already did leave town."

There was a storm blowing across his face. Sometimes people respond well to coaxing, but I sensed that he might be diverted by another interruption. Little movements broke up the unflappable image he usually presented. He took off his jacket. Then he was up, walking down the bar to get an ashtray. I'm sure he did it to show me his gun in its shoulder holster, but to make what point I wasn't sure. My dad no doubt loved that tough-guy thing about the Reverend.

Just then, four more bank board members walked in in four more good suits. Gary slipped on his jacket, but they must have seen the gun. Who are these people who make deals in bars with pistol-carrying partners, and what the hell was I doing in the middle of it?

I stood up and Gary introduced the suits. One was a member of dad's board, who I already knew. But the others were strangers to me.

We hadn't even moved past the pleasantries or sat down at the table when the bartender called Gary over.

When he came back he walked close enough to me that I had to step back.

"We just got a call. Federal Deposit Insurance Corporation liquidators are at the bank," he said. He looked wild. "They're closing the bank."

"So, that's it then."

CHAPTER · 34

When I got to the office, Adrianne met me at the door. "Federal regulators are at First," she said. "They plastered masking tape on the automatic teller machines and padlocked the front door."

I tossed my notebook on the desk. "That is why the insiders were running and why Cecelia wanted the story told. And we missed it."

"We didn't have the whole story yesterday. Don't have it yet today. But we will."

"What time is the bank meeting?"

"They're meeting at five."

What was the edge I was picking up in her voice?

"I talked to the president." She stopped. "He said I would be the one to represent the paper."

"I'm the legitimate representative of the *Journal*. We should both be there."

"That's what I told him. He said the publisher of the other Harlem paper is an essential part of this community."

"And I'm not?"

"He said, based on your attitude this past week, they can't even be sure they can trust you to keep what they discuss off the record through the weekend."

"Did you remind them we don't have an edition coming out until next week?"

"I tried to convince him we should both be there, but he wouldn't budge," she said. "He said the way this information is handled could mean the difference between life and death. You look terrible, by the way."

"You don't look so great yourself."

I left her, and put on my sunglasses and walked back to 125th Street, feeling the heavy public humiliation of not being on the scene of real news in the making.

"Hey, wait up." It was John Johnson from the television station. "Pearl Washington, are you on your way to the meeting about First? The word went out today that FDIC liquidators are moving in to take over the bank. They sent me up to see what you all are doing about it."

"If you hurry," I said, "you can probably catch some of the people who are doing something about it."

"Will you be available later, if I need to check some of the background for my story?" he asked.

I handed him one of my father's cards and wrote Adrianne's name on it. "Call this number and ask to speak to my editor, Adrianne Sinclair."

He was staring at the tape on my nose and the discoloration and swelling that was probably showing below the glasses, and he looked like he was going to say something. But then he probably thought better of it.

At the downstairs door to the upstairs office where the meeting was being held there was a bevy of representatives of the powers-that-be—the second tier, once or twice removed, eager, mostly young, dressed for effect in their conservative power suits.

"I want to know what we're saving if we save this bank," said the wisecracking sister who represented the white governor. Her life-long ties to Harlem gave her the kind of access he paid her for. But apparently not access to this meeting.

The congressman's rep stood outside the door in his secondhand glory.

"Pearl Washington!" Reverend Garrison said and he smiled at me as the guard at the door ushered him in and closed the door against me and John Johnson and the small crowd of B-team others.

And I was left with the dawning realization I had just missed the Harlem scoop of the decade, perhaps the century.

CHAPTER · 35

A wake is a place where an information junkie might overdose, and I was looking forward to having at everyone in the same room. But first I had to take care of my business. I was talking to myself as I went to get the money I had pushed through the hole in Cecelia's wall into my house. While it wasn't mine, it also wasn't exactly Ceel's. And it wasn't stealing and I was definitely going to pay it back.

And it wasn't there.

I crawled through our portal and ran my hand along the wall behind the cabinet looking for a sign that someone had used it. If someone did, they knew what they were doing. I had put the money there quickly when I heard Gary. But I made sure my side was tight when I went back the next day. So, who? How?

Next, I called Attorney Robinson.

"I hate to ask, but the *Journal's* money is stuck in the bank. Can you front me a piece of the payroll until Tuesday? We deposited a good little sum from Veteran's Day ads yesterday. But now it's stuck at First. I was counting on it. I've alerted some of my vendors. But there are the staff checks."

"Of course. Would a thousand dollars, do it?"

"Ummm. I was thinking more like five thousand. Some of them agreed to wait until next week when this mess is resolved. This is something to tide over a few of them."

"You don't have to impress me. If I remember correctly, you aren't paying any Lear jet money over there."

"But it's the long weekend."

"You're going to take almost all the cash I have on hand."

"If this is a hassle, I can gather together some cash from other sources. I was just trying to avoid putting all my business in the street."

"For five, I'm going to have to charge loan shark interest."

"I don't know anything about loan shark interest. How much interest are we talking about?"

"I'm joking. No interest if you get it back on Tuesday. Tuesday? I thought you were leaving this weekend."

"We're putting out a special edition about the bank. And we had to put off the reading of the will until Monday after we get the paper out. I'll move the money from my bank in L.A. when the banks open Tuesday after the holiday. Or, maybe, hopefully, what's left in our accounts at First."

"I'll give you the money tonight at the wake. Do you have that kind of time?"

"Tonight will be fine."

I left the house wearing my dark glasses and bought some Better Crust pies, which I left at the Miller's. Then I walked up the hill to Benta's Funeral Home where the clan had gathered to pay their respects.

Aretha was singing "Precious Lord" over the sound system.

I made a mental note to have Adrianne assign an article on the state of the funeral business.

As I walked through the room, I was reminded of the bebop and swing we piped in for Daddy's going home at Gary's church. I could almost hear it. My soul was stirred and I stopped to feel it, standing in one place for a minute, until I sensed someone trying to get around me.

Our Congressman touched my shoulder and paused before he passed. "Miss Washington. It's so good to see you back home. I love your movies. Gives Harlem the best kind of public relations—action with heart."

"Thank you," I said. And I must say I was surprised. He's good.

But he was already making his way to the next cluster of constituents as he passed through the room and finally stopped at the small group surrounding our bank president who was information central—the man with the world on his beautifully tailored shoulders.

I postponed going over to interview them and instead showed my home training by making myself walk down to the front.

Ceel looked weird—all fixed up to look like she was asleep, except gray and stiff and stuffed and surrounded by flowers. I turned away and spoke to the family who sat in the row facing her, accepting our sympathy. Mrs. Miller had been drugged, I think. She smiled a little smile to greet each of the people—are they called guests?—who stopped to give her their condolences. But the little smile frequently slipped, and a woman in white bent down to her.

She asked me to take off my glasses and her comments about my injured face distracted us a little.

Mr. Bell was sitting next to her. "Now we know what she was trying to tell us about the bank," he said.

"You always think there will be time to do the things and say the things," her mother said. "I often worried she'd have to take care of me in 20 years."

Mr. Bell got up and walked with me to one of the row of chairs in the back.

"I'm so sorry," I told him.

"I know. And I'm sorry about last night. Bobby must be desperate."

"Did you take the money?" I said without any of the preliminaries I had rehearsed.

To his credit, he didn't ask *What money?*

"You and Ceel were smart little girls. I was on your side when Elizabeth and Charles were deciding whether to let you have your hole in the wall."

"Where is it?"

"Safe for now. Elizabeth does not need to know about this."

"Cecelia was stealing bank money?"

He recoiled. "I would not say stealing. Not exactly. But there are people who will not be satisfied until they get it back. You do not need to put yourself in that kind of harm's way."

CHAPTER · 36

Some of the conversation stopped when Gary walked in.

He nodded to the Congressman and the bank president and made his way from the back, lingering, slowing down, speaking or nodding to the other mourners who had gathered to bury their friend, and the curious who had come so they could say they were there and so as not to miss anything.

When he finally arrived at the front, he was able to do what I couldn't do and knelt in front of the casket and spent some time looking at what they'd done to Ceel.

Mrs. Miller stood up and she and Gary held each other. When they separated, Gary walked back toward us, taking the time to touch people along the way, to lay hands on them who needed it, sharing the grief.

When he got to us, I asked, "Can we talk about the bank?" It was probably rude. But I didn't know how much time I had.

He took a few breaths and I caught something on his face as he performed a little smile. I know acting and that wasn't bad. The stripe in his bow tie coordinated with the flush on his face.

He said, "Your name came up at the meeting about the bank. Did Adrianne tell you?"

"We haven't talked yet."

"The president said this week has been more difficult because of your interference."

Mister Bell moved between us. "If you had been honest with us about what's going on at the bank, we'd probably not be in this shape," he said.

"In fact, I have a fiduciary responsibility to NOT report back what happens at First Amalgamated Bank board meetings."

"You don't understand that you get your legitimacy from us, not the other way around," Mister Bell said.

"You're hopelessly stuck in the sixties," Gary said. Then he said to me, "Also, by the way, you were mentioned again for publishing the bid list of 61 banks. First was offered for sale to those banks across the country."

"Some other bank is buying the bank?" I asked.

"Actually, no. Nobody would buy it."

"Is the six million dollars to purchase the assets of First coming in?"

"The money is coming in."

"Then the bank will stay open?"

"Unless some political decision is made. This bank is critical to this community. There's no reason to let it fold."

"I can think of some reasons," Mister Bell said. "Try racism and vindictiveness and pure down meanness. It's been my experience when crackers get to make selections, they select us out."

"Does THEY change, depending on the circumstance?" I asked. "Or is there a cadre of little men called THEY who are out to get us, like the Wizard of Oz, standing in the background, manipulating things in the ongoing plots against us?"

"Both," Mister Bell said. "The Wizard of racism is busy. We yell at him a little, win a little, and then we go do something else until we get mad again."

"Well, we're mad again now. Let's see if it makes a difference this time," Gary said, and he went to join the group around the bank president and the congressman.

Mister Bell pointed to the congressman. "And it's a way to punish him."

"Look at him. Is this what the civil rights movement got us?" I said. "Is another black congressman really supposed to do it for us?"

"We need him to do what he does."

"And what is that?"

"He brings home the bacon. He's now near the front of the line to get us our share of whatever they're giving away in D.C."

"But whatever they're giving away is not enough of what we need and he hasn't changed that." I had a mouth full of comeback; I had made this point before. "We don't even see him unless there's an election and many of his constituents don't even eat swine. If he's so good, why does Harlem look like it does?"

"He deals with an even stronger strain of racism than we do," Mister Bell said. "Don't underestimate him. Things are changing. I think it will look sudden. But the groundwork is being laid right now."

Attorney Robinson handed me a leather clutch. "Here's your cash. I expect it back on Tuesday."

I motioned to Adrianne and gave her the payroll. Then I nodded toward the president's group who were deep in conversation. "I need to join them over there while they're willing to talk," I told her.

"The president is not going to talk to you," Adrianne said. "You know that, don't you?"

"But he is going to say something quotable. How could he not?"

Mister Bell said, "Just remember, he had a hell of a job trying to find his footing in the quicksand he found at the bank. And I doubt he ever planned to get old and grey at our colored bank."

"Good quote. Can I quote you?"

"Of course. I'm on the record now that the secrets have all been told."

"Not all. We're going to publish a rich special edition Tuesday."

Adrianne gave me a thumb's up.

Mister Bell went back down to the front of the room to join Mrs. Miller in front of Cecelia. Gary said some beautiful words in a broken voice. Someone I didn't know sang "Amazing Grace."

And Adrianne was wrong, the bank president gave me a good quote: "Now you see what we are up against. This is a strong but battered community under siege. We need to work as one community with one mission."

CHAPTER · 37

The funeral on Saturday morning felt intimate to be so full of folks. Reverend Doctor William Garrison in white vestments put on a memorable performance from his oak pulpit, handed down from his father, in front of the backdrop of oiled wood, stained glass and draped velvet. He preached with just the right mix of gratitude for a good sister now gone and certainty of her redemption in the beyond. The sentiments were buoyed by the voices of the Resurrection Chorus, who had been called out to sing on a Saturday.

Cecelia would have approved and I was glad when it was over. He ended with a Rumi poem he said she loved: *But listen to me. For one moment, quit being sad. Hear blessings, dropping their blossoms, around you."*

I'm not sure how much more of it I could have stood. I moved to the back of the crowd filling the front of his church where I could watch the mourners file out. The crowd included Adrianne, Karl and Samantha from the newspaper.

And when we got outside, I stood next to Adrianne on the sidewalk, while the official mourners including what must have been out-of-town family climbed into two limousines behind a hearse full of Cecelia in her rosewood coffin under an abundance of floral arrangements. Behind them, the procession of cars waited. I got a chance to hold hands with sister friends and share about this and that we remembered about being girls together.

Viola was kicking her black with hot pink opera gloves and a Kentucky Derby hat with the veil of feather mesh covering her face. She left in her own black car.

Gary was among the last to climb in before the sad parade headed to some little upstate town to send Cecelia home at the graveside ceremony.

"Why aren't you going to the burial?" Adrianne asked me. "You are really family. And I thought Buddhists have a place for death."

"I have paid my respects as best I can. But I have something else I must do."

When the space was empty, I walked from the church down the hill. I was glad to be wearing my lace Miss Kitty boots rather than heels. They allowed me to swing through the park and cross St. Nicholas and Eighth Avenues, to join the living along the wide boulevard of Seventh.

When I found a working phone booth, I called the Reverend's community development office and got a message machine instead of any staff who might be there on a Saturday.

Harlem Village was in a storefront between a barbershop and a restaurant—both open at lunchtime. All the activity caused me to rethink my plan. The front office was visible through the big window and it was empty. When I walked around the corner, I discovered the back doors of all three businesses were accessible from an alley. The restaurant door was open and the smells were complex and meaty. As I fingered through a couple of the keys on Cecelia's heavy key ring, I heard pots and pans and running water and some yelling through the screen, in French.

I tried some keys at Gary's back door, and found the two that worked. Then I stood inside for a moment waiting for the alarm to sound. When it didn't, I moved quickly through the dark back storage room and into Gary's inner office behind the public room with the big window. Back there, it was kind of a mess of leftover Styrofoam cups and yellow legal pads. Every one of the file drawers I checked was locked.

But some of what would go back inside the drawers formed a cluster of clutter on the desk and tottering piles on chairs, and it looked like they might give up some secrets.

With all those movie scripts in mind, I went over and locked the door to the front office and began to take notes about what I was seeing, being careful to put things back where I found them.

I discovered several folders tagged *Harlem Journal* and closed my notebook and turned on Gary's copier and started making copies. Looking over the top of the machine, I saw two duffel bags dumped in the corner. Both turned out to be full of money in small bills wrapped in rubber bands in denominations from singles to fifties. I thought it was unfortunate because if they were the small dollars from Bingo or the tithing baskets it seemed like they should be treated with more respect. I was estimating amounts when I heard a woman's voice I recognized outside at the street door speaking to someone passing by.

I turned off the copy machine, put the money back in the bags and the bags against the wall and the folders back on the desk. I rolled my copies and stashed them in my tote as I was walking through to the back door. I looked both ways before I slipped out and locked the door behind me and went down the alley and turned around the corner.

As I often did, I superimposed on Adam Clayton Powell Jr. Boulevard sepia images of the days when pretty women and fancy men dressed up for the kick of strolling on Harlem's boulevards.

Until, suddenly, the time was now and the images were danger because a man in a sharp suit with a bandage on his face was walking in the distance toward Gary's front door, and I moved easy and slow into the doorway of a bodega and hated the rush of heat in my face at the sight of him. And when he reached the office door, Bobby Bop turned and shot his finger at me.

CHAPTER · 38

I walked over to Harlem Hospital and waited in Obsidian's empty room. At the mirror over the sink, I repositioned my mother's funeral hat, which I'd finally grown up enough to wear. When I had adjusted it at the top of the bandage on my nose, the veil covered my discolored eye.

I found a plastic water pitcher and put it on the table with red roses and ribbons of ivy in it—what I had been able to buy and pilfer on my way over. I made them messy so they wouldn't look like the stiff formations surrounding Cecelia.

Obsidian came back into the room wearing his street clothes. "Why is it only okay to give a man flowers when he's all busted up?" he asked.

"I'll remember to send you flowers when you're better."

"I'll be taking them home when I leave today."

"Do you think that's a good idea?"

"I just need rest. You can't rest in a hospital."

He got close. "Girl, come here. Let me see. Turn. Turn the other way. Take that net off."

I blushed warm. "It's a veil. It's my mom's."

"But how did you let it happen? Even if he had a gun, he had to get close enough for you to block him."

"I saw it too late and only dropped a little. Otherwise, he probably would have broken my nose."

"You say it isn't broken? So, you were lucky this time. And there will be no next time."

It was hard not to tell him I got a jab into Bobby with the throwing star. But, fine as he is, he's still the police.

"I'm sorry I didn't get to teach your guys to meditate Friday after they closed the bank. I'd like to do it when I come back," I said.

"We can do it tomorrow. Same routine. You come between shifts. I like that it will flow organically."

"Organic isn't the word I would use. Slipshod, accidental, not serious. This isn't something to throw at them. I want to be intentional about it."

"Next time. This time I want you to land on your feet like we do. Take them with you where you go. Your recent adventures will give you some credibility with them. Word is you're all over town being Lt. Summer Knight."

"No. I've been all over town being a reporter. I can't walk down the street without running into a story."

"You were arrested. You had a gun at your throat. You found a dead body. You were punched out. That's not walking down the street."

"I'm trying to figure out how the pieces fit together. For instance, you know it was Heavy who killed Cecelia. Somebody paid him to scare her. She wasn't supposed to die."

"If you had told me before, we could have pulled him in and he would still be alive."

"I didn't know it before. And you've been out of commission. And this session tomorrow still sounds like a bad plan."

"Sometimes plans can get in the way. It's not like you have to practice, do you?"

"Yes. I practice all the time. What I do is called a practice."

"Seriously. I want you to come now. What are you going to bring? Not any statues and flags I hope."

"A bell."

"Cool. The sound will allow us to focus." He smiled. "In fact, what about a siren? That way they can feel the stress you're going to talk about."

I didn't laugh and thought about it. "Interesting. Do you have one that's not so loud? I'm interested in how sound figures in your world, actually. Thank you for the idea."

"It's not my world. You live in it too. You just don't have to notice from your faraway Hollywood place."

———◆———

When I got over to Seventh Avenue, I walked up to Ruthie's and caught Riley and Joseph standing outside.

"When Mister Bell gets back, please tell him I need to talk to him. Tell him it's about Viola."

"Why don't you wait for Marcus at the repast?" Joseph asked. "We're going to pay our respects over at Elizabeth's house."

Riley said, "We didn't make it to Bentas. Don't like looking at dead people. You want a ride over?"

They waited for me as I walked around Riley's green Chevy van. I read the stickers on the windows from University of South Vietnam, School of Warfare; two ribbons, one yellow and one black; and a bumper sticker announcing, VIETNAM VET, PROUD TO SERVE.

In the center of the back window was a badge, crimson and gold for U.S. Ordnance Corps with text that read SERVICE TO THE LINE, ON THE LINE, ON TIME.

I took Riley's arm as he helped me climb in and let him close the door, kind of like stepping through a time warp to some other place where gentlemen live.

In the Miller's parlor, the mourners were eating and talking with their hats and shoes off, still waiting for those who were about the business of burying Cecelia. They were many generations. They were black and white and other. The men had established their own separate space in the back parlor. Women were in the front. Children were everywhere—some restless, some crumpled on laps or upholstered furniture.

I ate a little something.

C H A P T E R · 39

The phone was ringing when I got home, but it stopped by the time I unlocked and got in. I deposited my keys on the table by the door, turned on the small light and kicked off my heels. I walked across the parlor floor and picked up a beaded bird from South Africa, my gift to Daddy, appreciating the sweetness of the familiar.

I started to fix a drink and thought better of it and walked over to the dining room table where I sat for a minute before the phone rang again.

I let it.

Four generations of my people used to sit down to holiday dinner at this table when it was let out with the extra leaf. The earliest ancestors of the clan were staring down from frames on the walls. They were the subject of familiar tales I had heard for 40 years and I had expected one day to pass on to my own children.

The next time the phone rang, I picked it up.

Obsidian said, "I'm out of the hospital and I don't have any food in the house and I'm guessing you don't either. I thought I'd order us up some dinner."

"Thank you. But I'm not feeling like coming back out. It feels so good to be home."

"I caught you. You said home."

I laughed and relaxed a little. "I ate something at the repast."

"Then you can keep me company. Stay put. Give me an hour. Then we can finish our conversation."

"You should not be running around."

"I didn't say I was running over."

He lied. It was more like 30 minutes. And I barely got out of the bathtub in time. I arrived at the door completely covered in a jumpsuit.

His bomber jacket was draped over a sling and he placed his bag of Chinese food on the little table in the foyer. "Come here."

I fought against the thing in his eyes and lost. One arm was enough, as it turned out, for him to pull me close enough to kiss. Maybe not as much to pull, as to guide me, since I was already moving toward him until my mouth met his mouth and without a thought in my head, achieving my goal, as I felt him against me for a moment before I had to turn away.

"Does it hurt your face?" he asked.

"A little, and we have to talk."

"Yes, we can talk, *first*." He sounded as breathless as I was.

"It's not that funny."

It wasn't, but laughing is what all that feeling turned into.

"Are you going to be all right?" I asked him.

"Are you?" He touched the bandage on my face.

"I am. I always am," I said, feeling a little sorry for myself. "Sit down. I'll get us some real plates and utensils."

"Can we have a fire?"

"Sure." I started over to the fireplace.

"No. Let me."

"Can you build it with the sling?"

"Ha. You will be surprised at what I can do with this sling."

My refrigerator was barren now that neighbors had stopped dropping off the after-funeral covered dishes.

I piled plates and silverware and napkins on a silver tray and added two beers. I put the tray on the carved Haitian table, put Miles on the box, and arranged myself on the couch. And from there I watched him. A sight he was too.

It turned out he could make a fire with one good arm. Then he scooted me over to sit with the good arm next to me, and while I fixed our plates, his fire caught and blazed up.

"I see you're still a vegetarian."

"Yes."

"It must be hard to reconcile believing it's wrong to kill animals, and yet, you're a cop."

He put his chopsticks down. "I'm against killing people too."

"But, once you sign on, you're one of them. How can you stand it?"

"Can you do this tomorrow?" he asked. "I'm not bringing you in to meditate with my people as an outsider who is judging them."

"I'm not going to talk about the politics of the thing. I'm going to show them a practice."

"The shift changes at 4. You can start at 3:30."

"Which reminds me," I said. "We need Al to put out the special edition of the paper tomorrow. Can you get him out?"

"We've picked him up twice in the past two days."

"He didn't really do anything, except he was at the wrong place when the bootleg gang was busted and he took Heavy in when he needed to hide and the fool brought the drugs in."

"Heavy needed to hide because he killed someone."

"How come you arrested Heavy at the collapsed building and

couldn't figure out he was the one driving the hit-and-run car? Don't you guys take fingerprints?"

"There was no reason to compare those prints. And processing fingerprints is labor intensive. Takes weeks. Only way we get it done quicker is if it's a big case. They've started a process to put them on a computer so we can compare prints. But the crime lab still has to hand-compare inked print cards. And they were partials, which makes it harder."

"I'm surprised," I said. "It's faster in the movies."

"You all make that shit up. You need to get back your results and bust the bad guy before the credits roll."

"I need to get my notebook," I said. "This is important. I don't want to get this wrong."

"You are not going to quote me."

"No. I wouldn't. It's background."

"I want to stop talking about it for a minute."

CHAPTER · 40

"Stop talking?"

I was thinking he meant we would just look at the fire. But maybe I knew what he meant.

His mouth was so sweet. But I had to pull away from him.

"Does it hurt to kiss me?" he asked. "I'm sorry."

"It doesn't hurt. But I can't breathe through my nose."

"Me neither, he said. "Help me. Why do you have on all those clothes?"

I stood up and unzipped the jumpsuit which I must have put on to make it hard to do this thing. I stepped out slowly and he watched me.

I was careful, remembering his shoulder, but compelled to move onto his lap as though we were magnetized. And once there, there was no way I should have been able to feel the heat from his hand brushing my body so gently like that.

"Talk to me," I said. "I'm leaving again; you have someone. What do you want from me?"

"Do you want to hear that I love you? Do you want to hear that I have thought of little else except this since I saw you again?"

I wasn't sure that's what I wanted to hear. But my body was responding.

He shifted a little. "You always fit right there. It's where you belong."

I needed to look at his face in the firelight with its angles. The little break in his hairline marked a wound, years old. The small scar in his eyebrow was new.

I kissed him again.

"You're going to have to help me with this," he said.

"I kind of like having you a little helpless."

"I'll show you helpless."

I got to undress him and we ended up on the rug with soft wool and chenille throws, in the arc of warmth from the sighing, popping fire.

"I'm really going to need your help now," he said and opened his good hand with a condom in its wrapper in his palm.

I was hungry for his textures and tastes and smells and sounds. I was careful of his shoulder, but his hand and his mouth made me careless about everything else.

Then, I felt him playing with me, touching me, then backing away. He had me too close to pay attention then and without thinking about his shoulder or any of the other things I needed to worry about, I was on top of the sweetest . . . and slowly down and back up again. And I watched him, loving that he was mine at that moment.

And, finally, I remembered this man, the memories becoming waves rushing into places so deep they had not been touched since the last time. Then, when I was happy, yes, laughing, with the remembered joy of him, I heard myself gasp as the waves touched new places, and what was water became fire, then became clear, pure light.

And when I noticed again, he was pulling the throw over us.

He said, "If you want to say something, you might say, welcome home daddy."

"No. I can't. That hurts. I don't get to say that ever again. My Daddy is dead."

Then I broke down. Finally. I was not heaving and gasping and trying to close the space where my father was supposed to be like I did when the grief first hit me. But he was slipping away. I could feel the place that was as wide as the ocean emptying of anger and everything else. And I was surrounded only by love. It's where a boy lived who was not my Daddy, and then he was, and he did the best he could do, and he loved me and he learned to mother me. And I was feeling all of the sweet, sweet sadness of it.

And Obie was holding me and I was holding on.

"I've got you," he said and his voice broke.

• ◀ ▶ •

I woke up in bed to feel his arm pulling me closer to him, and when I looked, I discovered he was still asleep. I loved that he wanted me closer in his sleep and I snuggled against him, wrapping one leg over his, and dozed off again.

The next time I woke up he was sitting up.

"Good morning. How is it now?" he asked.

"Me? I'm spent. Empty. Cried out I think."

"It was beautiful to feel you feel your father. The deep sadness in your eyes makes them smoky."

He ran a fingertip just beside my lips.

"Thank you. I thought I couldn't let it happen, couldn't feel it without being swept away. You kept me safe. How do you feel? Are you in pain?"

"I took a pill. It's okay. I can take it," he said. "Come here."

I looked away.

"You can't regret this?"

"Not yet."

"I think our lovemaking may be foreplay," he said, "to reestablishing the intimacy of our long friendship."

I laughed. "I think I love you because of how your mind works, maybe even more than because of how your body works," I said.

"Speaking of how my body works," he said and kissed me. But then he moved away. "What time is church?"

I looked at the clock. "I'm going to hear what Reverend Garrison has to say at the 10 o'clock service."

"What do you expect? Some homily about the money lenders?"

"I don't know. But I have some questions that will be part of the bank story."

I stood up and wrapped my mess of hair into a twist, which I secured with a barrette.

"I like it wild," he said.

"I noticed."

"No. I mean your hair." He stood up. "Let me go first."

I kissed him when he came out of the bathroom, and I went in and locked the door behind me. I scared myself in the mirror. It was going to take some doing to make myself presentable. Not for Obsidian. My lover knows me. But the church folks expect Sunday-go-to-meeting.

When I opened the door, he was almost dressed.

"You're in a hurry? Do you have time for coffee? Or, are you going to church with me?"

"You locked the door," he said.

"I have used up almost all the flexibility in my schedule this morning," I said. "I need to take some notes before I interview Gary while he's captive in his church and can't run away from me."

"Had I been allowed in the shower with you, you would not have been out of there perhaps before noon. Do you remember our shower scenes?"

"Yes. And I remember baths in your mother's decadent tub."

"Mmmm. Yes, there was that. But I was imagining you standing up and feeling the skin on your back, wet and slippery and fragrant against me."

He turned away and I smiled. I had the advantage of keeping secret the effect his words were having on me.

"You aren't using enough makeup to cover your eyes?" he asked.

"I have shades for church. But I think this look is perfect for our meditation at the precinct."

"You might be right. But it's going to take more than a black eye to fit in with my men."

"I'm not trying to fit in because I'm wounded. I'm fitting in because we're all in this together. I believe we're interconnected."

"Please don't preach to my guys."

"Trust me."

We walked together downstairs and embraced at the door.

"You've got 30 minutes starting at 3:30. I've told them you were coming. You'll get a chance to make a pitch to grab a few more. But right now, you've got 4."

"Four is a good start. Thank you. This is important. Thank you."

I watched him walk away.

CHAPTER · 41

I had to stand at the back of the church up the hill and wait for the processional to enter. I watched the good sisters turn to follow the right reverend as though he was the light.

The man who will always be the church's second in command led the service, while Reverend Garrison sat to the side of the pulpit, which had been his father's before it was his. But when it came time to preach, he's the one who got up. I took out my notebook, making one part of the rustling sounds of the church settling in to hear him.

Gary was acknowledging the elected officials, sports figures and entertainers who had shown up. He also asked visitors to stand and asked those who were visiting from foreign countries to stand again. There was a horde of them; most came in the long buses parked on the wide street or the narrow avenue outside.

"The offspring of slave-holders are expecting us to hold a funeral today for our bank. They know how we love to sing songs about home-going. I preached such a sermon yesterday for our good sister Cecelia Miller, and I'll preach such a one Wednesday for our good brother, Clarence Jackson. Clarence was one of the talented young people who we have been trying to rescue from the war that's going on out there. We can't afford to lose any more of our future."

"This community is too familiar with the abomination of parents burying their children. Marjorie and Ephraim Jackson are here and Elizabeth Miller is here. Be sure to show them your love. But today, I've got something for the progeny of slavers. I've got a sermon about self-sufficiency and a message about fight-back."

"We call on everyone of goodwill to provide financial and heart support in this effort to save our bank, our First Amalgamated Bank. At this time, in this moment, we have come together and will resurrect the dream of First's founders who solicited early deposits door to door. Our bank has risen from the ashes more than once."

He looked strong, in charge, a knight well-suited to fighting for our good cause. The chinks in his armor didn't matter in the fortress of his church.

"We must now also admit we have taken our bank for granted. But at this time, I remind you, urge you, no entreat and provoke you, to support her, to call and write and fax Washington DC. Let the people in government know this community is behind its bank and we demand they give us time to bring her back. The fax numbers and phone numbers are on the lists we will pass out as you leave the church."

He waved at the ushers at the top of the aisles.

"We only have one more day. Make sure to sign the petitions and take some with you and get them signed and bring them back by early tomorrow afternoon. We will get them to our Congressman's office to make our demands in the name of our congregation and our community."

On this Sunday, Gary's church was the place to be, and the press was broadening his audience in the packed church beyond the congregation and the tourists.

Then he yanked me back.

"Before we close, I want to say the name of one of our long-time heroes, Charles Washington. Charlie told the truth and made things happen. His daughter Pearl is here. She is doing the work of her father. Give her some love."

At the end of the service, I walked through people I knew and people I didn't, making connections, hugging and hand-holding.

At the back of the church, I could see the reverend through the wooden doors just outside his inner sanctum. I joined a hodge-podge of people, the men and women of the church—deacons and deaconesses, secretaries and Christian congregants.

I told the secretary I'd like to see the reverend for a moment and I showed her my expired *Harlem Journal* press pass. She didn't look at it.

"He'll be right with you, Pearl Washington. Come with me."

CHAPTER · 42

"He's in God's hands now," Reverend Garrison said to an aged couple, stooped in their Sunday best. "We will only say the words on Wednesday to help us acknowledge as a community what you already know so well."

He turned to me. "Pearl Washington, I want you to meet Clarence Jackson's mother and father. This is Pearl Washington, now publisher of her father's *Harlem Journal* newspaper."

I reached out my two hands, one to each, and thought to say, "I'm so sorry. It's like the reverend said, we are devastated to lose our precious future."

I didn't tell them I knew how they felt because my father just died. I hate it when people do that because then it's about them and the dying and the grieving is personal. I also didn't tell them I was the one who found their boy dead.

"Thank you," his mother said, and they left the office holding hands.

Gary closed the door to the vestibule sounds and anybody who might be curious about what he was up to. His bow was blue, tied under his stupid beard.

"That was sad. Heavy's parents are so old."

"I'll need to talk to Pearl alone, Deacon," he said. And the man who was busy at a table piled with blueprints on the other side of the office left without a word.

"They had Clarence late and he has been quite a handful. But we thought he was coming around. And now this. If you're writing a story, make sure and write about Clarence being an artist and funny. I talked to him the day he died. We talked about how hard it was for him and how much support he was going to need. But he didn't say it was life and death."

"You talked to Heavy? Where?"

"He called me but he wouldn't say where he was."

He motioned me toward a group of chairs as he answered the phone and said something into it I couldn't make out. His rosewood desk caught my attention. I think I know why he had replaced the huge oak monster that used to take up almost half the space. Sitting behind his father's desk would probably have felt like sitting behind my father's—like our feet wouldn't touch the floor.

"If you have a question, ask me now. I need to get this over with. Sunday is not my day of rest."

"What I want to know about is Viola and Ceel money laundering. I saw cash in your office and I found wrapped bills that had to have been withdrawn from the bank. And I also saw another list of bank withdrawals, but from companies with music names like Louis Armstrong Associates. Fake companies. They were money laundering and that would require a cash business to channel the money through. Was that you?"

"If you've got Viola, you've got your cash business. My deacons and board make sure I don't have access to money. Our church organization is structured to keep me from temptation. And my money is not just what I get out of the baskets on Sunday. It's also government and corporate philanthropic money. I have to keep a shit-load of records."

"So you knew about it."

"I'm not admitting it even happened" he said.

"We both know it did."

"It's your job to spread rumors, not mine," he said.

"The *Journal* does not print lies. That's one of those urban myths," I said. "Like the myth about your bank supporting community businesses."

"But we do. When nobody else will. We're just not in the business of throwing money away."

You don't get one of those bank jobs by running off at the mouth. He stopped. "When will this story come out?"

"In Tuesday's special edition about the bank with follow-up stories in the regular edition on Thursday."

"Ceel used to say she wanted to have your life," he said.

"Don't tell me that. That's terrible."

"She was going about it all wrong."

"What do you mean? What would be a good way to go about having somebody else's life?"

"That's not what I meant. But it's an excellent question," he said. "Harlem is getting ready to be a destination. The white boys can't do it without us and we can't let them take it from us. Pay attention. Ceel isn't the only one. In fact, Viola and your father were expanding the Kit Kat. It's a jazz spot that already pulls the downtown crowd. I heard she was there at the hospital with you when Captain Bailey was shot. That's all right. She made your father laugh."

"He loved to laugh."

"And she played the hell out of the damsel in distress," he said.

Gary's image was sure and annoying.

He paced. And when he turned to me, he said, "Viola got Cecelia in more trouble than they could get out of. She was trying to extricate herself when she was killed."

"Extricate just herself? What about Viola?" I asked. "Did her partner agree it was time to give up all that money?"

"Viola and I both disagreed and tried to get her to stop calling attention to the bank. It was foolish and dangerous."

I hated that I had to keep the notebook in my bag.

"Cecelia had a fiduciary responsibility. She broke several confidentiality agreements with these leaks to the newspaper and these charges. She was on my church board and I was on the bank board. We were interconnected in so many ways."

"And that's how she figured it out."

"She got it wrong. And you have stolen property. I'd be careful if I were you. I'm warning you. The bank's board of directors is not going to sit still for this."

"If you don't tell me something else, I've got me a story."

"You can't do this. Especially not now. Not this week. We need to be sure the bank looks as good as it is."

"Why not now?"

"Off the record?"

"Don't tell me anything you don't want in the paper."

"Then we don't have anything else to talk about."

He pushed a button on his desk. The big deacon came in and Gary told him, "See Miss Washington out."

I stood against the wall in the corridor and was writing down some impressions and images while they were fresh. Until the presence of someone who had stopped in front of me caused me to raise my attention from the notebook to the space my body was inhabiting.

"I'm Janice. Obsidian's," pause, "friend," she said.

"I'm Pearl." I gave her a semblance of a smile.

She raised a perfect eyebrow. "Of course, I knew you were Pearl. Thank you for being there at Harlem Hospital with him. I couldn't get out of my commitment and get a flight back until this morning and I hate that I was away when he needed me."

"He's better, mending, it seems," I said.

"Yes. He's coming home from the hospital today. I'm going over after church. I'll tell him we met."

"Yes, do tell him that."

I watched her walk away and wondered if there was something else I should have said. And, if so, what it might have been. Perhaps my best over-the-top Hollywood scream.

"She's gorgeous, isn't she?" I jumped but didn't give the reverend the satisfaction of seeing my face and walked the other way.

CHAPTER · 43

I was not in a great mood to lead a meditation on calming the mind. And they were not loving me at the 28th Precinct, where I got to be the interruption to some of them going home.

Obie told them the 30-minute training session at 3:30 would include meditation. And they didn't have to stay or come early for it. I had about six, sitting on chairs. And a few wandering in and out.

"You know me. I'm Lt. Summer Knight. I play a cop in the movies in my other life. I also teach meditation."

"I know some of you have a martial arts practice and already know that in order to be a complete martial artist you need to know your mind as well as your body. But knowing your body as a tool is different from knowing your body as home. That self-awareness will help us find calm and compassion, including for ourselves."

"That's the WHAT of what we're doing."

"The WHY of this experience is that stress is the mind killer. This is a stress reduction exercise. When stress lands in your belly and chest and neck, it will travel with you to the next experience or the next person you meet, and it will follow you home. But you know that."

"That brings us to the HOW of what we're doing here."

"On the street, you're always aware of what's happening around you. And just for this moment, I invite you to turn that incredible awareness inside. Fold your attention into your body. Breathe. I'll walk you through what I do and you can join me. Try it. See what happens when awareness touches your body. Where it lands. How it changes."

I rang the bell.

"Hearing. How did that feel? Don't say it out loud. Just be with the feeling. Hearing the sound of the bell landing and touching your ear."

"I'm sleepy," somebody said. Somebody else laughed.

I gave them and me a moment of silence.

"How does sleepy feel? No judgement."

I heard a deep sigh.

"Just breathe. Know the in-breath and the out-breath. Don't think about it. Be aware of how the breath feels entering your nose and traveling down the body to the belly."

I took them through a body scan from the top of the head, the face, jaw, shoulders, arms and hands, front and back upper body, belly, and only got a laugh when we got to the butt.

"Shhh," somebody said to whoever was chuckling.

We made it through the 20 minutes. I rang the bell.

"How was that?"

"It was nice. It felt good. But it doesn't have anything to do with me. Maybe if I was somewhere else. Not here in this precinct."

"He's right. It's not real," another one said.

"Can you imagine anything more real than us sitting here right now? Everything else is not happening yet or it happened already. We're just left thinking about it right now. Our thoughts are with us. Our thoughts are in the present. So is the breath. So are our feelings, the sensations touching our body. They come, they go, they're not permanent. And they're not who we are."

"Can you recommend any books?"

"I'll send a list."

"Are you coming back?"

I looked over at Obie who had walked in and was standing in the back.

He told them, "Not right away. But I want to know how that landed for you. I'll talk to any of you who want to talk about it over the next few days."

Afterwards, one of my meditators came up and thanked me. He called Obie "Captain." Another one just called him "Bailey."

Disrespect. Interesting. Obsidian's jaw tightened and he walked away from us.

CHAPTER 44

I waved walking to avoid talking to the Sunday guard standing at the back of the lobby and took the elevator to the *Journal* office suite. Seeing Daddy's name was a tiny, quick comfort. In fact, Daddy could have just stepped out to take a walk—nigger watching he used to call it. It was meant with love that was as deep as it was perverse. I shared enough of it to make me glad to be home and then glad to be running away again.

Samantha was beaming. "Imagine. We've got two so far. But you know these things come in threes."

Her body-count didn't seem to need or deserve a comment. I only shook my head as I went to my office to call Roger in California.

"I found out some more news," he said. "Not about the bank. But the movie theater complex is real. They're trying to decide which empty lot to put it on."

"Those lots have been empty for a long while waiting for a deal like this. They call it land-banking. Are you sure?"

"I got it from an insider."

"You're good at this reporting."

"People like to tell me stories."

"Me too, actually. That's how I landed in the middle of that bootleg bust. I found myself in the middle of two murders too."

"You don't sound like an interested outsider anymore."

"Harlem is a universe of small worlds. Everything is connected. It's amazing."

"When are you coming home? I thought you were only going back East to take care of your father's affairs."

"I'm staying through the Veteran's Day holiday and to see what happens when the bank opens on Tuesday."

The pause took a little longer while I decided whether I needed to say it and if I could bring myself to do so. "And, Roger, I've spent some time with Obsidian."

"The old boyfriend." He whistled. "I thought he was in the hospital."

"He's mending."

"Spent some time? Did you forget the precepts? The training to avoid sexual misconduct is on the Buddha's list of five training precepts."

"Damn Roger. What kind of passive aggressive bullshit is that? You're not mad?"

"I'm mad. I need to squirrel this information back up in my hidey hole to see how it really feels. And you need to stop." He slammed his phone down.

"Can I make a suggestion?" I jumped. It was Samantha standing in the doorway.

"You have quite an annoying way off sneaking up on a person."

"That's how I do my job."

"You are not using anything you heard on that call. Understood?"

"Damn. I walked in too late. What did I miss?"

She was not a convincing liar.

It was almost an hour later when I looked up from my screen to notice the street sounds from across the room through the windows, opened a crack to let some air in.

I reread what I'd written. Then I had to unfurl my brow and relax the grim line my mouth was making. Okay.

I printed both my stories and the caption and popped the floppy disk out of the computer, feeling like Fred Flintstone for having to carry by hand what could have been done so easily electronically. Maybe Daddy was selling the paper; inefficient was not like him. And not telling me?

It was a bittersweet moment to take the familiar walk down the long hallway. I walked slowly and noticed the plaques and framed pages lining the dull lime walls.

DISTINGUISHED NEWSPAPER PUBLISHER CALLED HOME
Charles Washington
November 21, 1925 to October 22, 1990

JESSE THROWS HIS HAT IN THE RING

WHY DID MEDICAL EXAMINER REMOVE DEAD MAN'S EYES?

SUMMERTIME

The first was the latest. The last was a front page with two wide-eyed kids, who were called colored in the paper then, sitting on the curb eating watermelon. The other half of the page was full of bathing beauties busting out of bits of bathing suit.

A Bootsie cartoon by Ollie Harrington floated in a wooden frame.

During the *Journal's* heyday in the 50s and early 60s, there were foreign correspondents on staff, at least monthly a highly salacious front page, and at least once a fistfight in the newsroom.

But Daddy had let the paper drop to second place. A man once thanked me at an awards dinner because the *Journal* gave him the idea for his successful business. He produced plaques. The *Journal* is full of photographs of the bestowing of plaques for a job well done, money well spent, or for the hell of it.

In its silver frame was the quote by Russwurm and Cornish from the opening editorial of the original *Freedom's Journal,* from which Granddaddy had taken the name of his newspaper:

We wish to plead our own cause. Too long have others spoken for us. Too long has the publick been deceived by misrepresentations, in things which concern us dearly . . .

CHAPTER · 45

When I got to the production room, the floorboards creaked, but there was no one in the large room to hear it. Without Al, our layout was uninspired, but the articles crackled. Handwritten at the top of a page was one headline:

Fed Shuts Down Our Bank

Below the fold was a banner.

INDEPENDENCE INSIDERS
WITHDREW $$$$ AND RAN

Adrianne walked out of her office. "Damn! This is some prize-winning journalism happening here, if I do say so myself," she said.

"I like that we blame the distant racists in the banner and question our own below the fold. It will be a sort of dueling of ideas about who is responsible for what happens around here. It'll be a nice counterpoint."

I showed her my draft. "This belongs in the local section too. It's not finished yet."

SOME DEPOSITS WON'T BE CLAIMED

"I finally figured out the significance of all those withdrawals from companies with music names. They're fake. Cecelia was money laundering. That would also explain some cash I found and the money she was spending on art and vacations and things."

"At least it isn't stealing," Adrianne said.

"You don't seem very surprised."

"She didn't hurt anyone."

"You really believe there's a hierarchy of illegal activity?"

"Seriously. Who did she hurt? Tell me how it worked."

"It was probably illegal drug money they had to clean up by running it through a cash business where it would blend in and then into a bank. She would be the insider who shuffled the money through a made-up bank account, always less than ten thousand dollars at a time."

"Why the hell was Cecelia keeping lists?" Adrianne asked. "You don't keep books of money laundering."

"Hell if I know why, except she was always the one who was keeping track of the details. And we still don't know how much," I said. "There were only withdrawal amounts written next to the companies and no balances. And I don't know which cash business she used to channel the cash through. Both Gary and Viola have cash money coming in and both had a connection to Heavy. He was the bouncer at the Kit Kat, and Gary said Heavy called him when he moved into Al's."

Adrianne said. "Damn. Make sure to leave what I'll need to get the rest of the story when you go back to Cali."

"There will be a lot more to it, but I'm betting we can get the opening act of this story in the can now."

"You've really gone Hollywood, Pearl. Your movie might go into a can, but the *Journal* goes to bed. Remember?"

"Of course, I remember." I said. And as I walked along the long drafting table, I dropped into images of me sitting in the publisher's office with my books and notebooks while Daddy talked to people. Or in the production room where I would get blue and black ink all over myself from climbing to see. And dressing up, starting as a little girl, to sit in the audience with him or watching him talking to people, asking and answering questions. And after, he would answer mine.

At the end of the row, I pointed to an empty square, forlorn, on an inside page. "Do you have a good photo for this one?" I asked.

The small headline read:

CLARENCE (HEAVY) JACKSON
MAY 10, 1968 TO NOVEMBER 8, 1990

"His parents are sending some pictures and an obituary," Adrianne said. "I thought we might go lightly with the news about the drugs and the murder."

"I like what you've done. You're putting the bank stories outside and the other news inside. That way we don't lose any momentum waiting for the regular edition."

"In fact, we don't know whether or not this stuff is connected. I miss Al. He would have made one of his presentations out of this edition. Made it pop."

"Do you think Al can stay clean after this week of being arrested and threatened and worse?"

"Don't start that shit, Pearl. Don't judge him. Your father hired him when his chances were slim to nil for staying off drugs. But he did, and now he's excited about his new life."

"I don't rule out recovery. But I do know it's a long shot."

"Most things worth doing are," she said.

"I know it's a long shot because I have the experience of watching people get straight and not. Don't lecture me."

"You'll forgive me for doubting you understand," she said.

"And you do?"

"Perhaps we should talk about something else."

I went home and drank some liquor. The drinking did what it was supposed to do. It took some of the edge off. I was thinking a few more drinks would maybe dull it completely.

I'm not sure how soon it was before the doorbell rang. The space was sort of out of focus as I walked over to see.

It was Obsidian.

CHAPTER · 46

Monday morning, I woke up on the couch downstairs. When I picked up the edge of the duvet, tentatively, I was relieved to see I was in my PJs. When I tried to sit up, the head was screaming and the stomach was swishing and I wished I was dead.

"You slapped me."

I whirled to face him, which was a big mistake, and I had to stop and hold my head in my hands.

"Obie. I don't remember. But I'm glad if I did."

"You're lying. How could you not remember?"

"I'm not the liar; you are. I thought you said you would wait for me."

"Janice is what I've been doing while I've been waiting."

"I wish I wasn't so sick, so I could slap you again."

I got up and when I got back from the bathroom, there was a Coke and a Gatorade on a tray on the table.

"What are you doing here? Did you undress me?"

"I was afraid you'd go out."

"I'm at home. You can go now."

"I am afraid, disappointed, sad. How did this happen? Is this how they do it in L.A.? Get all drunk and stupid?"

"Is this what we're going to do now? Talk about my drinking instead of grief and broken promises?"

"This is bad. Your father's pancreatic cyst was related to his drinking years ago. You have a family history."

"Mind your business."

"You're right. My mom used to get like that. I know what to do, but not if you don't want me to. It's too hard."

"You need to go see about your girl Janice."

"I'm going."

CHAPTER · 47

Samantha and Adrianne greeted me at the door to the office.

Samantha announced, "The hard thing about this week's column was finding a secret everybody doesn't already know. But I did it."

"You need to see this," Adrianne said.

We walked to the production room and found a beautiful front page laid out on the long drafting table. Al was sitting at the other end wearing headphones.

REGULATORS SET TO THROW
BAIL-OUT $ IN HARLEM'S FACE

After a long Veterans Day weekend, more than 6 million dollars in oral commitments came in to purchase the assets of First Amalgamated Bank. But the banks where that money would come from will still be closed by the 7:00 A.M. deadline after the holiday. And the FDIC will have to give community leaders time—those extra hours—to convert those letters of credit into cash.

"We won't technically have the cash in time," board member Reverend William Garrison said. "But we have the pledges. And since when did banks stop accepting promises?"

The subheads set up the other related articles.

WHO BUYS A BANK?

The F.D.I.C. has not found a successor bank that will buy First, after offering it to a bid list of 61 banks. Because of the savings and loan crisis, nobody is rushing to buy a bank.

ACCOUNTS CONSOLIDATED:
BALANCES OVER $100,000 NOT INSURED?

Kiss and Tell, by Samantha

Rumor has it that accounts at First Amalgamated Bank with balances over $100,000 won't be insured by the FDIC if the bank folds. They have been insured at other banks that closed. And, also, significantly, separate accounts held by the same depositor will be combined and some of those totals will be way over the insured amount. Such accounts could include nonprofits, community development groups and churches, and the United Negro College Fund. Continued on Page [__].

"Samantha? Why is this running as your gossip column?"

"There's a New York State law that charities with multiple accounts are trust accounts and each account should be insured for the whole amount."

"Then if they do this, it's illegal."

"Yes. And I can call out an illegal action in my column where it's not exactly news yet. I've done it before."

Adrianne said, "I agree. We've got a page one story. We're going to run it with Sam's question mark and rumor-has-it lead."

I walked the length of the long drafting table that stretched down one side of the suite's largest room and waited for Al to finish making a cut with the mat knife to place an ad on a half-page.

I nudged his arm.

"What a relief you're out of jail," I told him. "We needed you to tighten up this special edition. It looks good."

"What a relief is right. I think the cops were as surprised as me."

"Tell me about Heavy and about those movies I saw at your apartment. They had to come from a postproduction house," I said.

"I spent some time on the coast getting straight. Met some people. You'd be surprised."

"Was that what Bobby was talking about when I saw you at his black-market factory?"

"Bobby was giving me a tour of what I needed to do to get enough copies produced to make some real money. He needs me to get those movies. His are mostly unwatchable, shot on camcorders with the audience sounds. And I needed him to distribute. He has people in Florida and Texas and Chicago."

"He said you owed him some money. Is he the loan shark?"

"Sometimes. He's the only banker that won't throw a small businessman like me out into the street."

"What about Heavy?"

"He called himself street muscle. He ran errands for money."

"Murder?"

"I'm surprised as you. Didn't know he had it in him."

"Somebody paid him to hit Cecelia?"

"When you find out who, you'll know something."

"So, tell me who. He must have told you."

"You sound like the police. Like I told them, he figured the only way he was going to get out of it was to man up. And I sure the hell don't want anybody to think I know who they are."

CHAPTER · 48

Samantha walked over.

"I'm fat with column copy this week. And I'm thinking I'll let you all help me decide what secrets you want me to publish in my second column. Let me see. How about Pearl Washington is selling the *Journal?*" she offered.

"No." Adrianne was firm.

The rest of the staff turned to us.

I spoke slowly, realizing I was moved. "I am Charles Washington's daughter and I want you to know that whatever happens, whether there is a sale now or later, whether I end up here or not, I'll look out for you. You all are the best. This paper gives this community what it wants—what's happening and why, a laugh and a secret. And it gives them what they didn't know to want—the truth without the excuses. I am privileged to work with you, all of you. Adrianne and I have been talking over these days and she will be in charge until I get back and we can figure this out. I will not have someone else second-guessing her."

"Thank you again," Adrianne said.

Sam tried another story. "What Harlem cop is back with his first love."

"No," I said, louder than I meant to.

Sam smiled at me and tried another one. "What bar owner and grieving widow can now give her full attention to her outside man?"

"Viola was running around?" I asked. "Who?" I felt the sour in my stomach rising dangerously. "I wonder if Daddy knew?"

"Yeah, I kind of doubt he wouldn't know. How are you going to be tipping around Harlem and nobody knows? But it doesn't matter who. I'm not one to use names in these cases."

"You don't have to run it."

"I don't have to. No. I never *have* to run any of this stuff. But I probably have a better one. How about somebody paid somebody to scare Cecelia Miller and he accidently killed her? Then they had to kill him because he wouldn't keep his mouth shut. They found out where he was hiding."

"Yes." It's a trio with Al. We all agreed to the hit-and-run story.

"He told me she stepped off the curb," Al said. "She was supposed to be on the curb."

"And Al, you won't say who paid Heavy?"

"I don't need them to think I know."

"I love that Sam's column can hold all the suspicion and rumor. You all can get to the facts soon. But we don't have to wait for them."

"I need a drink," Adrianne said.

"Me too. But I need you to wait for me at the Kit Kat. I'm going to Jackson & Robinson for the preview of what Dad's will has to say."

"I'm coming too," Al says. "Attorney Robinson told me I'm in the will."

"He didn't tell me. But that's good. Adrianne?"

"Yes. I'll see you at the Kat."

After the printer's messenger picked up the special edition, the staff started dispersing to catch the last hours of Veteran's Day.

Adrianne said, "I know you've asked yourself this question. But what are the consequences if we're wrong about the bank? And about all of it?"

"We're not going to miss another scoop. The Wizard of Racism that Mister Bell talked about is out from behind the screen. We need to bust him."

When they left, I got daddy's 10mm out of the false bottom of the side drawer in his desk and loaded it.

But I noticed the possibility of once more stepping into a place of dishonoring the mindfulness trainings I had vowed to live my life by—a life where I was aware of how I showed up, where I could pause and intend no harm and hear the voices of others who shared my intention.

But here I was running around taking all manner of unskillful actions. I had harmed Bobby Bop, but as carefully as I could, and that was without a gun. It was true, as Roger said, my lovemaking with Obie could I suppose be called illicit sex since we both had commitments to others. I had consumed many substances that made me confused. Thank goodness, Ceel's money was gone before I could steal it for my payroll. And at least, so far, I had only lied a little.

I saw myself slipping and sliding around my intentions and aspirations as I put the gun back in the drawer.

CHAPTER · 49

My father's widow made her entrance at Jackson & Robinson in a red suit and kid gloves, and when Attorney Robinson went over to greet her, her smile blazed at him in the dim conference room.

When Robinson returned to the head of the conference table, there was a smudge of red on his check.

Gary arrived and walked to the other side of the room.

A secretary handed out an asset list.

"What the fuck is this?" Viola waved the sheets at us. "This is what he has for me? An insurance policy? And only enough to finish the work we already started on the bar." She turned to Robinson. "What is the date of this?"

"This was drafted in the last month. A very recent accounting."

Viola's chair fell against the floor as she stood up. "That stingy bastard. What the hell? After all this time?" She turned to me. "I'm going to be getting all the money back. If you fight me, I'll win. I'm his wife."

"I'll tell you what I know about you fighting me," I said. "My father probably didn't leave you the money because you were cheating on him."

She started to cry. "We married so I could take care of him and he was supposed to take care of me," she said. "You don't know how it was. I promised him I would tell him if it got to be too much. He would not look up and find me gone without a goodbye. It's hard to be with a person who was sicker and longer than we expected, especially when it's someone who is used to being in charge. But to do that, I needed to get away for a few hours. I had to find comfort, to get my shoulders rubbed, to have a glass of wine. Then I was able to come back and love him."

When she walked out, Robinson spoke into his intercom. "Stop Viola. I'll be right there. Excuse me." And he left us.

Gary, who had also stood up and started to follow her out, sat back down.

"It looks like everybody wants to save the damsel in distress," I said.

"She put the H in hustle, and I think your father and I both liked that about her," Gary said. "But it is also her undoing. She and Cecelia were in way over their heads."

CHAPTER · 50

When we got outside, Viola was sitting on the bench, waiting.

"Pearl! Come. Sit down next to me," she said and patted the seat with her glove.

Al waved and kept walking.

I sat down next to her. What the hell. It was at least some part curiosity to see what she was going to get up to next. And it was the opportunity to get at some of what was on my mind.

"We didn't use your name in our money laundering story," I told her. "You were the cash business the dirty money was funneled through to Cecelia to deposit in the bank."

"I was wondering how long it would take you to figure it out."

"When did she start withdrawing money from the bank?"

"Why do you ask?"

"I found some," I said.

"When I found out, I stopped depositing the money they brought to the bar. Then she nutted up on me. Started giving information about the bank to Samantha for the newspaper. She said she was doing it to alert the community to save the bank. But she alerted our partners as well. And she said I was the one who was reckless. I spent some. It's true. But not enough for her to nut up on me like she did. I didn't trip on it too tough. She was spending money too and she had more reputation to protect than me."

"How much are we talking about?" I asked.

"Tell me how much you found," she asked.

"Over $400,000 in bank-wrapped bills."

"Where is it?"

"It's safe," I said, which was a half-truth based on trusting Mister Bell.

"Good. That's good. But she said she couldn't get it all out the bank without raising an AML alarm."

"AML?"

"Anti-Money Laundering. But she didn't write down any balances on the list you gave me or those insider lists, only withdrawal amounts. So, I don't know what we're talking about as you put it."

Funny how things land. "You saw the other insider list? That was in the safe. You broke into my office. That was you who shot Obsidian."

"I didn't mean to shoot your man, Pearl. I was shooting to miss you and he was just there."

She turned on the tears again which gave me a minute.

"I need your help," she said. "It was an accident. And Obsidian's going to be okay. Can you forgive me? I need your help. I need that money."

She was a psycho, for sure. But she was no longer my problem. Now, I was only worried about Virginia.

"What I will do is take Virginia when they arrest you for shooting Obie. And the house is mine. Do not mention it again."

She was struggling to get up.

"You don't have to tell?"

It occurred to me that I wouldn't be called an accomplice since

I was on the other side of the room when she shot a New York City policeman.

"No. I won't tell."

But I needed to ask her some things while she was free to talk, before she was arrested or worse. "Wait. Tell me something," I said.

She sat back down. "Can we make it quick?"

"It needs to be quick now. I'm not sure I'll get another chance to ask. You were here when I was not. You spent all that time with Daddy. I want you to tell me some stories. What was he thinking? What was he doing? How was it? Did he still make his little sunny-side up egg breakfast with sausage and toast and jam almost every day? Was he disappointed that I wasn't here?"

"Oh, my lord. Please don't doubt that he loved you. He was proud and happy that you were following your dream. Although he thought you might take some roles that were more serious." She smiled, but saw something in my reaction. "No. He liked what he called your early career. He missed you all the time. But that's the love."

We held each other for a moment. I was stiff as a stick to her attempt at cozy suffocation.

Then we took a gypsy cab from Jackson & Robinson to her house.

During the silent ride, I practiced what I was learning to touch her suffering and mine. I said to myself, "May you be free of danger, both external and internal. May you meet the changing nature of your heart with equanimity. And may I too find equanimity and peace."

Practice. It takes practice.

CHAPTER · 51

While Viola was fumbling with her keys, a pair of muddy red sneakers caught my eye, sitting on top of a plastic shopping bag lined up so neatly, the way we do in the city, in case somebody barefoot came by. It seemed odd to me.

"What's that?" Viola said.

"Looks to me like sneakers in a Barney's bag," I said.

"You're not bringing that garbage into my house. Put it back."

Mr. Bell came to the door. "Viola told me you might be coming."

I moved the sneakers behind the cans before I followed them inside.

Mister Bell said, "I'm Virginia's favorite babysitter. She's upstairs. She fell asleep. Tell me what happened."

I let Viola tell the tale: "Charlie didn't leave me anything but an insurance policy. He only left enough money to finish the bar."

Mister Bell whistled and we walked into the kitchen where she started making drinks.

And I did some reporting.

"How much money laundering cash do your partners already have, Viola? Bobby got some from Al's. And you gave him money that was in duffel bags in Gary's office Saturday after the funeral."

"You're good," she said. "With the $400,000 Cecelia left, I don't think we're so far off.

Mister Bell turned to me. "Pearl. You told her about the money?"

"And you didn't?"

"No," Viola said. "He didn't say anything about having money when I have been frantic trying to figure out what I was going to do." Then she turned to Mister Bell. "You should have told me," she said. "You know I need that money."

"Tomorrow, we'll give them the bank bills I'm holding. And if there's some different figure they have in mind, I think our story is it's stuck in the bank," he said.

"You know, that's the truth," I said. "Even if the bank's still in business tomorrow, nobody's going to give you any money out of an account called Louis Armstrong."

Mister Bell smiled. "Those company names were silly. Are silly. But the fallout is no joke. This is very dangerous. Viola, you don't want to face your hooligan partners alone."

"They're coming here?" I asked.

"Later. I thought we would talk tomorrow," Viola said. "But they decided they wanted to make sure I didn't leave town or some such foolishness before they got their money. I won't be alone. Bobby won't let them hurt me."

The name of the man she was cheating on my father with was one more thing that fell into place.

"Let me take Virginia. She does not need to be here with Bobby's people," I said.

Viola said, "She stays with me. You don't know. She's a real trooper. She wants to be with me."

Mister Bell looked from one to the other of us. "Viola, I can't imagine you are going to get all of Charlie's money you want. Not now or in the long term. I think you all are going to be in court for a long time."

"If you fight me, I'll win," Viola said to me. "In New York, the wife is entitled."

"Not after you get arrested for shooting Obsidian," I told her. "I won't be the one to tell. But you're not getting out of this one. There won't be any fight over the house. And Virginia will come to live with me."

Mister Bell put on his hat and coat.

"I'll be back," I said. "Don't wake her up. I have people waiting to give me a goodbye drink at the Kat."

When we got outside, I said, "She's quite mad."

He tipped his hat. "I'll owe you that drink."

And he walked away.

CHAPTER · 52

I went across the street to the Kit Kat Klub. Al, Adrianne and Samantha were all there. A piece of Miles' "Sketches in Spain" was on the jukebox.

"Sam said. "You look frazzled. Al told us what was in the will."

"I get the house and instructions about money for the bar and the newspaper. He gave me a way out. But not any time soon."

"You had to be an outsider to go after those stories. And you had to be a badass to walk across the no trespassing signs," Adrianne said. "I like that in a person."

"I'm not as outside as I like to be. I've made a point of not getting involved in Miss Viola's business. Until tonight. I'm not sure Daddy would want her dead unless he could do it himself."

"Damn. You're full of surprises," Al said.

"I know. But she was here when I was not. She made him laugh. And they did business together—music business with this bar—his second favorite thing after the newspaper."

"She is not the helpless victim, you know," Samantha said. "The sister knows how to get into trouble, for sure. But she can also get herself out of it or find someone who will."

"She asked me to help," I said. "I'm not sure what that means and whether I want to do it or can do it from the coast—even if that's where I want to be. This trip has reminded me that there are places to go and things to do besides making the same movie over and over."

"Shhh."

Viola came in the front door and we watched her glad-hand the groups of drinkers as she walked through her bar towards us.

I said, "And I'm really interested in finishing the bar makeover."

People welcomed Viola into the rather wide circle of their personal space, and she must have held court for ten minutes before she finally almost got to where we were. She was jumpy, wired, like she was on something. Is panic a controlled substance?

A large fierce woman stepped between us and her attention slid back and forth. Sometimes she eyed me while she continued her conversation with Viola.

"You know we always have a nice spread. I want to let them know you'll be there. I want my youngsters to see a woman doing business for herself and not for some man. I did call your office number and the bar. But I know they don't tell you things."

It came out all in a rush as if to keep her from being interrupted.

"You know I love your dinners, but I think I'm out of town next weekend. I'll check and someone will call you."

She was being dismissed and she didn't mind.

"And Pearl. You need to put the story in your daddy's paper."

"We put in the announcement. Did you see it?"

"Little bitty mention. I saw it." She looked like she smelled something bad. "We get a big crowd. You should send somebody."

"Send a photo and they'll print it."

She sniffed at me, thanked Viola again and again, and backed away, actually bowing a little.

"You're good."

"She's been giving those dinners since I was one of her youth. That plaque's going to cost me some money."

"Cheap at twice the price if the money really goes to the children."

She waved her hand as if to swat my words away. "It does. But I didn't come here to talk about her young people. You left before you said good night to Virginia. She wants to say good night."

I said, "Viola, I really need you to get Virginia out of there. She could get hurt."

"She's staying with me."

To slow her down and make the point that I don't respond well to being summoned, I finished my new martini slowly before I followed Viola outside. We stepped off the curb as allowed by the traffic light and I did the thing we all do as I checked to establish I had the light as I continued across the street. The car kept coming. I jumped onto the sidewalk in front of me and turned around to see Viola back up. But she couldn't turn in the heels, so her movements were jerky and awkward, like she was waving at the car. It kept going after she went down.

I took off running down St. Nicholas Avenue as the Chevy dodged the cars blaring their horns when it took the light. Lt. Knight would have had her gun in her hand by then, ready to shoot out the tires. In fact, she probably would have outrun the fool. But I didn't have the gun in my bag. As it was, I only got close enough to see there was no rear plate before he sped away, leaving me to go back and face the second real life traffic death I'd witnessed off-screen in my whole life and all in the same week.

But when I got through the few people who obscured her, I found Viola alive and sitting on the curb, dabbing at her eyes and smoothing her clothes and hair.

"What's broken?" someone asked. "You done really pissed somebody off."

"Nothing's broken," Viola told him. "I fell. He didn't hit me."

I stared at her and allowed the short breaths left after the run to land and settle. And from the place in my gut, the awareness turned into a clear understanding of what had just happened.

A witness got my attention when he pointed at me and said, "Did you see her run down the street like she was going to outrun that Impala? Damn. Go ahead on Lt. Knight."

I gave him the thumbs up.

The witness helped Viola get up but the rest of the group who had gathered around her were already dispersing. She didn't have to convince the police to let her leave the scene because they never came.

"This is serious now. They're trying to kill me," she said to me. "Or, scare me like they tried to scare Ceel. We need to talk about how you can help me get out of this terrible mess."

"Oh, hell no," I said. "I'm not helping you do anything. That car was aiming at me."

"You've always thought too much of yourself," she said.

CHAPTER · 53

When I got to the Kit Kat, Sam asked, "How's Virginia?"

"I never got there. A car just aimed at me. Viola said they, whoever they is, was trying to kill her. But, why would they? She's the one with the connection to the cash."

Al said, "And nobody's going to kill the owner of a bar who owes them money."

"Exactly. She must have decided she needed to get everything my father left, and with me out of the way, she would."

"That was a short détente," Sam said. "And, by the way, she needs to find a new weapon. This car shit is getting old."

"Why don't you tell Captain Bailey?" Adrianne asked and motioned to Obsidian who was walking over to us.

"He thinks I'm making up a case against Viola because I'm jealous. The jealousy thing has been true. But at this point I would not want to be in her stilettos."

"Shhh."

"I heard there was a bon voyage celebration going on." He paused. "I don't see celebration in your faces."

"We were talking about Viola."

"Daddy didn't leave her anything in the will, because she had some boyfriend," I said.

"That's a shame," Obsidian said.

"Pearl, don't you have anything else to tell Obsidian?"

"Not yet."

He said, "Pearl? I'm not going to buy you a drink. You've had enough. I just wanted to say goodbye." He raised his glass of sparkling water and juice. "Until we meet again."

Then he steered me away across the room.

"Pearl, can you avoid getting drunk tonight? I want to come over to talk about it, whatever it is you don't want to tell me."

"I'll tell you this. I didn't invite you here. How dare you show up trying to shame me in front of my staff."

"I'm not trying to shame you. I'm telling you something you need to hear to be safe and well."

I paused and let the thought form and how to say it.

"If you want to keep me safe, you should know Viola came after me just now. I'm not making this up."

"Is that what you were going to tell me? And I'm supposed to arrest her on your hearsay?"

"I know better. I'll get you the evidence you need."

"You can't say things like that to me."

"Why? Because what? You'll do your job?"

"No. Because I can't let you get in the way of me doing my job."

"Can't let? What does that mean? Are you going to arrest me?"

"As far as I can tell you haven't done anything to warrant arresting you."

"Not yet," I said.

———•———

I waited for Obsidian to walk away, and, since Mister Bell had not come to the bar, I went to the pay phone. I retrieved the matchbook I guess I had stashed for just this moment and called Ruthie's.

Mister Bell wasn't there. When Riley came to the phone, I said, "I'm going to get Ginny out of Viola's because I think she's in danger. But I need a distraction. Can you set off some small explosive or something?"

"What makes you think we could do such a thing?"

"I don't have time to play games. Your ordnance expertise is all over your van and I've heard your combat stories."

"We won't do anything until we hear from Marc. But if we did, what are you suggesting?"

"I was thinking, there's an alley behind those houses. Can you make some noise like when the building partially collapsed? I'm remembering the shit-load of firemen who showed up at the property two doors from Vy's the other night. And can you do it without putting that building or the garage at risk? I need less destruction. But I need confusion."

"We could do that. We'll wait for Marcus, but I know he wanted to get Viola out of trouble for Cecelia's sake."

"Viola is the trouble, actually," I said. "I'll need 60 minutes from now. I'm counting on you."

CHAPTER · 54

When I went back to the front of the bar, I told my posse, "I want Ginny out of there. Will you help me?"

"We ain't Charlie's Angels," Adrianne said.

"There will be an explosion and I'm thinking I'll get her out during the confusion. She and I can drop down to the alley behind Vy's."

Adrianne said. "That's some comic book shit."

"I know. But it's the only thing I can think of right now. And it will work. I'm going in, but I need a distraction. Her partners who are waiting to get their drug money out the bank will be there. I don't have time for an elaborate carefully laid out plan."

"Then they'll try to kill you, and what? They do?"

"That's not the plan. Here's my keys. Right after you hear the noise, we'll be in the alley. Take Ginny to my house. It will be the safest place for her."

"Hell yes, you need a distraction," Adrianne said. She stood up. "I'll help you. But I'm not thinking about going in there. And neither should you."

Al stood up beside her. "You need our help. Call us your fans. Call me one of the Angels. We'll wait in front, in the shadows. If you need anything, make a sign at a front window."

"The sign will mean to call Captain Bailey. Okay? Don't come running in there after me. Promise me."

Al made a noise that had no humor in it. "Something else you should know if you're putting yourself in the middle of this. Heavy told me Viola is the one who paid him to aim that cab at Cecelia."

I felt it drop. Cha Ching.

"He said she told him she had something for him to do she couldn't trust anyone else to do for her. And he couldn't tell it. He would want to because a boy brags. But a man holds his business close. Heavy said he told her he would show her how much man he is if she had a night or a weekend to give him." He shook his head. "I'm going to miss that crazy brother."

"Damn. I wasn't even looking to solve the first murder. Money laundering was the trail I was following after I saw those bills from the bank at Ceel's and then all those small bills at Al's and at Gary's."

"I'm surprised it took you so long. You never did like Viola," Al said.

———•———

When I got outside, I looked both ways, all ways, as I crossed the street to Viola's.

Standing at the street door with its wrought iron gate, I was thinking that the situation reminded me of Al's the few nights before, except this time, as far as I knew, the folks inside were still alive.

I figured out which one of the extra set on Daddy's key ring was to his girlfriend-wife's house. When I got inside, I could hear her in the kitchen in the back singing. Loud. While the sound of a truck lumbering up St. Nicholas Avenue covered the old house protesting, I walked up the stairs.

I stopped one flight up to wait for some more noise and looked in at Viola's suite of rooms. Her bedroom was painted a sumptuous deep blue-gray and the Chinese deco carpet added mad color. Something red was hanging on the back of the door in dry cleaner's plastic.

Once I got the accompaniment of another truck clanking and the welcome bass from some car speakers, I moved up the stairs to the top floor where Virginia was sitting on her canopy bed reading.

"Auntie Pearl? I have some cool Band-aids. Does your face hurt?"

I put my finger to my lips to keep her volume down. "Hi baby. It doesn't hurt any more. Are you okay? Are you afraid?"

"I'm not a baby and I'm not afraid."

"I'm going to take you over to my house because I don't want the company your Auntie Viola's getting ready to get to see us. You can wait there. Will you come with me?"

"Is Auntie Vy coming?"

"Yes. But you're going first. We'll hear an explosion in the alley in about 45 minutes. We'll leave together. But if I have to leave before you, I want you to run downstairs and out the window on the parlor floor. You know the routine. I've heard about your adventures."

"Yes. I know how to get out."

I leaned over and kissed her on her head.

"Why do you run away?"

"I don't run away. I just visit my friends. Auntie Vy is not home at night."

"How do you climb out the window?"

She pulled a rope ladder from under her bed.

"I use this when I have to get back in. I drop down from the window on the parlor floor. It's unlocked. The fire escape makes too much noise."

"Why'd you throw away the red sneakers? I saw them sitting on the garbage cans outside."

"I didn't. Look. Here they are."

I found out Viola had company when the volume of the music dropped and I could hear her talking. And it occurred to me it was not likely to be the kind of company that would be happy to see me.

I looked at the time. I had 35 minutes before I would get the cover of noise and confusion I was hoping for.

I could hear the conversation from the ground floor and then a new tune, loud, on the box.

"I'm going now," I told Virginia. "Will you come?"

"It's a good thing Uncle Marcus already took his suitcase. He asked me to watch it for him."

Pause. "What suitcase?"

"He left one in the closet but he took it when he was babysitting me before Auntie Vy got back."

She looked very serious and her eyes were big when she came to me for a hug.

I could hear the activity below us in the distance. I waited for the accompaniment of a truck rattling up St. Nicholas Avenue, more traffic, and then a siren to cover the sound of our footsteps moving down the stairs and the protests the old house made. I followed Virginia's lead and we made our way across the room along the wall at the edge of the floor, and we tipped over to the back window.

We stopped when the noise stopped. When another siren filled the space on the avenue, Ginny hooked the rope ladder over the sill.

She climbed out a few rungs and then she dropped down into the alley. I climbed down most of the way and I dropped down and landed in the alley behind her.

I saw a man standing in the shadow and grabbed Ginny and turned to run.

"Whoa. Where are you going?"

It was Adrianne in a baseball cap.

"I thought you were a man. You have my keys. Take Virginia to my house."

"Why don't you come with us?" Adrianne asked.

It sounded like just what I needed to do. But I said, "No. Whatever is going down needs to go down here. I don't want them at my house. Just see about Ginny for me."

"You take good care, girl," she said.

We got to the alley opening and I watched Adrianne and Virginia catch a black car. I told the driver my address and stood for a minute and waved.

CHAPTER · 55

"Don't turn around. Walk!" I heard him speak at the end of a shuffling sound that caught my attention too late. I was feeling mildly surprised and mostly resigned. "Bobby? Now what?"

"Lt. Summer Knight, you're getting ready to get real ugly."

He pushed me back towards Viola's house with one hand around my arm, while he held something at my back. There was no way I was going docile on him, but breaking away wasn't an option if it meant getting shot.

He pushed me again. "I said walk."

When I turned my head, I got to see the bandage on the damage I had caused when I cut his face with the throwing star. And he watched me register the knowing and jabbed something hard into my ribs. I didn't give him the satisfaction of any more than my groan to acknowledge how it hurt.

My brain was dancing through my few choices. The sidewalk was clear, and at the same time I hoped for one of the neighbors to witness and report, I didn't want anyone to be hurt as the drama unfolded.

The hand around my arm tightened and I could feel the other arm moving behind me.

"Turn around. I want you to see this."

I turned around.

"It's a nasty thing to cut somebody's face," he said.

He had holstered his gun and he swept with a dramatic flourish to open a knife, which left his middle open.

I drove my knee into his groin hard enough that he closed down on himself. Even with my injured rib, he was at the disadvantage and I took the gun out of his holster. Still, I had to back up quickly after I took the knife to steady myself and be in the position of holding the gun on him.

"You won't shoot me," he said.

"The hell I won't."

But I can't say whether I would or not because Viola came out through her parlor floor door.

"Please get off the street. Get in here. Where's Virginia, Pearl?"

"She's safe."

"I'm not through with you," Bobby said. "Know that I owe you."

I pointed his gun at him until we got to Viola's kitchen. Then I let it hang heavy against my leg and kept my distance. She looked at it and handed me my vodka and OJ.

The back of her hand was covered with scratches, and long welts and scabs also showed red and brown on the skin up her arm.

When she handed him his drink, Bobby took it with one hand and with the other arm brought her to him and they kissed.

"So, you like them young. Daddy must have bored the hell out of you."

"No," she said. "When he was healthy he could get down. We had a bunch of fun."

I had a little speech to make, whether I felt like it or not. And I did not. But I said, "Viola, you were right about your Chicago audience. Some of them were disappointed when you didn't show up

Thursday night for the Black Women Business Owners Festival. It was Thursday night Heavy was murdered."

"I thought you said you were calling me from Chicago when you told me where the money was," Bobby said.

"You were my last secret, darling. Don't listen to her. Thursday is when I got sick and had to cancel my presentation. There are people who saw me in Chicago. She's wasting our time with this."

"If she called you and told you to go to Al's, then she set you up for a murder," I told him. "Because Heavy was dead in there. And I'm betting those sneakers in the shopping bag behind your garbage cans probably fit the footprints I saw in Al's backyard, Viola."

"Oh please. No doubt those were Al's own footprints in his own backyard."

"Or, how about you made them when you came back to town and went to Al's dressed in a red track suit? People saw you. You must have been desperate."

She reached into a kitchen drawer and pulled out a gun she pointed at me. "Give me that," she said.

I let Bobby's gun hang against my leg just a little longer. It was my welcome companion. Then I laid it on the counter.

Bobby started for it.

"No. You stay there," she said and turned her gun on him.

"Vy. Vy. You going to shoot me girl?" he asked and laughed.

"You don't have anything else I need. You're the last mess I have to clean up."

"So, now I'm a mess? Ain't that some shit?" I felt a little sorry for him.

"More like a loose end. If it wasn't for you, Charlie would have left me most of his money in the will. I was counting on his money to pay back whatever cash I can pull together to get out of this mess. I need that money."

"You also need me. I've bought you the time with my partners to straighten out this bank confusion. And tonight, I aimed a Chevy at this one. You can't do this without me."

He was moving toward her when she shot at him.

"I won't miss again. Sit down."

He sat on the edge of a chair and she sat down on the other side of the kitchen but with her gun still pointed at him.

"You know, desperate is such an unattractive word," she said. "I had to wait for Heavy to let me in to Al's apartment after I rang and heard the rustling. I was tempted to wave at him when I knew he could see me outside around the curtain that was moving just enough. But I didn't wave. I'm not the type on a good day. And this was not a good day."

"He was wired and he was high from what I had the cop man deliver. He said it helped with the pain. He said his face hit the steering wheel. He took a pose. I suppose it felt like a tough guy pose from where he stood. It looked foolish and pitiful to me." She leaned a little forward. "And he was not dressed for travel."

"He took some of the money out of my little rolling suitcase and released the bills from the rubber bands. He said he was glad they were small bills and they would be easy to spend down south where he had some family. But he needed more, because it was one thing to drive a car at somebody and keep on going. It's another thing to have to cover up a murder and keep ahead of the cops."

She leaned back. "It was strange how in those few beats it was a relief—when I knew for sure what I had only anticipated. I told him I would get more money and to leave the door open so I could get back in. And I showed him the surprise I brought him. We shared the joy because we both wanted him good and high."

She looked at me directly. "I gave him time. And when I went back in and walked into the bedroom, he was unconscious. Then I heard someone outside. It must have been you Miss Thing. I couldn't tell if he was still alive, so I hit him with the baseball bat and ran out the back and climbed over the fence and landed in the bushes on the other side and got all scratched up."

I interrupted. "And you couldn't get the suitcase over the fence, so you called Bobby to tell him there was money at Al's and to go get it."

"That's your story. But how do you like this story, Pearl?" Viola said. "Bobby shoots you with his gun. And you shoot him with yours. You two are the only ones who know."

Although, I must say I always had the instinct there was something off about her damsel-in-distress act, I still had a hard time imagining Viola was capable of this level of evil. She shot Obsidian? She paid to put Cecilia in mortal danger? And, within a matter of days, this latest information was more like a wrinkle. She killed Heavy with the baseball bat. And now, she was getting ready to kill us.

"You are multi-tasking like a motherfucker," Bobby said, laughing absurdly for a man who'd already been shot at once.

"I'm not armed," I said.

Bobby bought me some time because he had pulled a small pistol out of his pocket and he aimed it at her.

At the same time, we heard the sound of the explosion, Viola shot him. She ran up the stairs.

"Call an ambulance," Bobby said.

"I will," I told him. And, using all the chops I'd learned as an actress cop, I ducked and ran, hugging the wall. When I got up to the landing I saw Viola going out the window and I heard what sounded like gun shots at the front door.

I climbed down the ladder to the alley.

CHAPTER · 56

I backed into Viola. She pushed me away.

"Did they do that?" She pointed to a van where it was moving to exit the alley. Next door to her house, the burnt remains of the wooden box covering the generator was still smoldering.

"Riley and Joseph said they could do it. It was clumsy," I said. "But I couldn't think of anything else to do to get Virginia out. I hope his friends call Bobby an ambulance."

"When did you take Virginia?"

"She and Adrianne took a car just before Bobby grabbed me."

We both wanted to get out of there and she had the car, so I caught her keys when she tossed them.

"Hurry."

"Who says it's hard to find new money," Mister Bell said, as he and Al walked out of the dark. He was carrying the Louis Vuitton speedy bag full of money.

"Marc! We're going to get Virginia," Viola said.

I walked to the front of the car. "We've got to get out of here," I told them. "I think Bobby's partners are in Viola's house. I heard them shooting at the door."

"No. They're not," Al said. "I was waiting outside. There was two of them. When we heard the explosion, they shot at the door lock and broke into the house and then ran back out and took off down

145th Street. The good news is, they are in Bobby's red Cadillac. Easy to find."

"If Bobby told them where Virginia is, they'll know where Viola is going to be. Come with us. We need to go." I held the car door open.

"It looks like you have this under control," Al said. "I'm not going to be standing around minding my business when the police show up. Let me see if I can get home without being stopped." And he walked to the alley exit and away.

Mister Bell said, "You go. I'll ride over with my boys. Their van is on the street. That was a neat little explosive ordnance event wasn't it? They called me, and I told them to go on ahead and blow some stuff up. They put a cherry bomb in the generator's gas tank and stuck the fuse in a cigarette. When it burned down it blew and then they put out the fire. Easy."

He took Viola's hand. "Virginia is a smart little girl. She'll be okay until we get there." He hugged her.

I thought I heard a backfiring vehicle and Mister Bell became a weight on Viola before he slid down to sit.

"Oh, my God."

"Get in the car," he said and pointed to Viola's window.

When I looked up, I saw Bobby Bop was sitting facing the window, his big gun in one hand propped on the window ledge. We watched him fall over.

"I'm okay," Mister Bell said. "You go see about Virginia. I'm good. Take this."

Viola reached for the bag with the money and stopped. "I need you to carry that bag," Viola said. "I can't manage it. I hurt my leg when I dropped off that stupid rope ladder. It's too much for me with this damn leg. Hurry."

I picked up the money bag with the intention of throwing it into the backseat of her Buick. And to make room, I pushed aside rags and tools and other junk someone must have been using to work on the car.

I drove us to the alley's opening, where there was a fireman blocking our way.

I recognized him from the night the house two doors away imploded, and I rolled down the window.

He remembered me too. "We have to stop meeting like this."

"Have you been careful?"

"Always am."

"I need to get to the street. The fire is out but I need you to call an ambulance. Two people are hurt back there. One is in the alley. One is in the building next to the one with the burnt generator. The window is open and he has a gun."

The fireman moved out of our way and we rolled out of the alley and onto St. Nicholas Avenue. The traffic was stopped to make way for another fire engine speeding north up St. Nicholas.

I used the empty uptown lane to drive downtown facing the truck two blocks away and turned left just in time on 145th Street.

I turned right on Edgecombe Avenue and drove south to 137th Street, and then over to Eighth, where I found a space at the corner. I moved the bag into the trunk and I walked and Viola limped down the length of the street, barely avoiding one of the neighborhood cats, now a gut puddle, at the curb in front of my house.

I heard music and knocked.

"Who?" Adrianne said.

"It's me."

She opened the door and Virginia ran to Viola for a hug.

"I'm glad to see you too sweetheart. We're leaving."

"No. You're not." Adrianne looked past us to the street. "We've got babysitters."

I turned around to look out.

"They're sitting in the red Cadillac down the street. But they'll be back. They came in right behind us," Adrianne said. "They don't want you to go anywhere until they get their money tomorrow."

I walked over to the phone.

"It's dead," Adrianne said. "What money are they talking about?"

"We left it in the car. All that money and still not enough," Viola, said, "Virginia. We're going to get out of here. I'm not wanting to be sitting here with them all night. Seriously. They could do anything. Give me my keys, Pearl."

"Then I'm going with you," I told her. "It's not safe for you to be driving with your bad leg and with Virginia in the car. You're liable to hit someone in a crosswalk."

She looked at me and raised her two hands in a surrender and smiled.

Adrianne asked, "How do you think you're going to get out? They're not going to let you just walk out the door."

"I have an idea," I said. "Come with me. We're going upstairs."

"I cannot hang out any more windows," Viola said.

"No. We're walking out the door."

They followed me upstairs, and I moved the cupboard and opened the door to our portal into Cecelia's house next door.

"What the hell?" Ginny said.

Viola said. "Your daddy always said you practiced at being Lt.

Knight by playing detective with Cecelia. But I had no idea you were this serious."

After we crawled through, I told them, "When we were girls, we read that prohibition bootleggers opened the space between the top floors of these row houses and escaped through them when the feds came in downstairs. Daddy had a beam put in. We have been using it since we were kids."

Virginia said, "This is like C.S. Lewis in Narnia. The Magician's Nephew."

"You are such a weird kid," I said.

I carefully closed the wainscoting, and we walked downstairs.

Mrs. Miller walked out of her room. "Pearl Washington," she said and looked at us. "And a crowd. What are you doing using your hidey hole in the middle of the night?"

Ginny went for a hug and was unable to easily pull herself away. "This feels so good," Mrs. Miller said. "How are you sweetheart?"

"I'm good Auntie Elizabeth," Virginia said and made her escape.

"We have to go," I said, and I walked over to Mrs. Miller. "Do you have anyone here with you?"

"No. I'm waiting for Marc."

Before I could gather myself to figure out what to do about this terrible thing, Adrianne walked over and took Mrs. Miller's hand.

"You all be careful," she said to me. "I'll stay here."

I led the rest of us down the stairs.

The front light was off. I disabled a motion timer, using the chops I learned when we were escaping as girls.

I opened the street door slowly and looked out. Then, I stepped back. Two men were walking up my stoop next door.

"Come on. We don't have but a minute until they see we're gone," I said.

All three of us hunkered down and ran along the parked cars to Viola's car sitting at the distant curb.

The trunk was open and a man looked up. But I had to kick him to get him to release the bag he thought he was going to run away with. Then I had to kick him again when he tried to grab it back. I allowed the one who was stretched across the back seat to pull himself out of the car door with the broken window. And we watched them both run down the street.

"Just in time," I said and slammed down the lid to the trunk.

"Virginia, see if you can find space in the back."

"It's a mess back there," Ginny said.

I turned on the car and saw my company running out of my house.

CHAPTER · 57

I turned down Eighth Avenue and headed south towards Obie's 28th Precinct. A red light at 135th Street stopped me.

I felt the cold when Viola stuck her gun against the back of my head from the backseat. "Turn the car around. We're going uptown."

"You know, if I don't, and you shoot me, you'll be in a wreck and you'll not get anywhere you need to be."

"Where I need to be is at the church," she said.

"Everybody needs something," I told her.

What I needed was to take us to a precinct. If I turned left to the closest, the 32nd, so close, right down the block, Bobby's friends in the red Cadillac couldn't shoot us and take their money, and Virginia would be safe. Instead, I did as she asked and took the light and turned right on 135th and then right again on Edgecombe Avenue, heading uptown. I turned off my headlights and pulled into a fire hydrant space just past Harriet Beecher Stowe I.S. 136. Within minutes, we watched the red beauty speed up St. Nicholas Avenue where it forked along beside Edgecombe.

I stopped at the light on 141 Street and waited to turn up the hill.

"How are you going to get into the church?" I asked Viola.

"Gary's there."

"I knew it. What does he have to do with this?"

"He took some bank loans. He doesn't want the bank business

public. Makes him an ally even against his will. And he did love Cecelia."

When I saw red in the distance coming down Edgecombe, I ran the light and headed up the hill and got honked at but not hit. The Caddy was a couple of cars behind me as I drove past the park and City College and the church, and got to Amsterdam and turned uptown.

Amsterdam Avenue was an obstacle course. I sped north and, using my best Lt. Knight moves, managed to keep control of the car. I found a way around and through moving and double-parked cars and so many people on the crowded avenue who couldn't care less about our rush.

Stopped at a red light, I heard the window humming open.

"Virginia, don't roll down the window," Viola yelled. "Stop it. They're coming."

"I know," she said.

In the side mirror, I saw the red Caddy move into the empty downtown lane two car lengths behind us.

"Virginia. Stop," Viola yelled. "Virginia. Stop it."

When I looked in the rear-view, I saw Virginia, who must have been on her knees, with a big oil can in her hands and I watched her pour a full can of the oil in a stream out the window.

"Perfect. And now I'll turn," I said.

I took the light and the left turn on 153rd, just south of the cemetery and I watched in the mirror as the driver in the red car tried to follow. Instead of turning left, the car careened around on the oil and turned the wrong way. He must have slammed the brakes because it was spinning again to the accompaniment of much honking in the distance.

I didn't see them behind me on 153rd Street when I drove across Broadway and turned up Riverside or when I turned right on 155th Street. I turned off my lights and made a U-turn and took the parallel side street between the American Indian Museum and the cemetery, and I waited.

"Virginia, that was brilliant," I said.

"I know."

"What is this going to get you?" I asked Viola.

"I just need to get through the night. Once they get the money, I don't have anything else to negotiate with. They won't hurt me until they get it," she said. "But they will do whatever they need to do to get it."

"I am not going to be part of this," I said. "When we get to the street, I'll take Ginny, and you can go on about your runnings."

"You can get out now. And Virginia's not going anywhere."

"When I get to a real street," I said. "I'm not getting out here. Who knows who is under the drive in the dark in front of us. And Riverside is not a safe place to be walking around at night."

We waited some more, and I tried to bargain with Virginia. "Ginny, this is very dangerous. You need to come with us. Your Auntie Vy can handle things better if she doesn't have you to worry about. You have become a disadvantage."

"I can help," Virginia said.

I tried to bargain with Viola. "She doesn't need to hear about all of the bad you have been up to."

"No. She doesn't," Viola said.

"Let her come with me."

"No."

"Okay," I said. "Why don't I tell your niece some bedtime stories that will shatter her lovely innocence."

"No. Don't do that."

"How about the one with Cecelia dying on 125th Street? Or the one where Obsidian gets shot in the shoulder and how bloody it was and how much it hurt? Or the one about Heavy being hit upside the head? Or, maybe, what happened to Bobby Bop?"

"They were all mistakes," Viola said. "And then self-defense. In fact, they were all self-defense."

"You know that's bullshit."

"Don't be a bully, Auntie Pearl," Virginia said.

"I'm not making this up, honey. Those are bad guys in that car. We need to go to the precinct. We need protection."

Viola said, "They will not be on my side. No one will."

It was still quiet and dark when I made the U-turn and drove to 155th. I didn't turn on the headlights when I turned west back to Riverside and drove north. A car pulled out from where it was parked on the drive and followed us. When it turned on its headlights it showed itself to be the Caddy.

Riverside was too narrow and too dangerous. And even when we could see where we were going with our headlights, it was still too likely someone would come out walking or driving or on a bike and be hit.

The entrance to the Westside Highway was just in the distance ahead of me and I saw them in the rear-view mirror when they pulled into the right lane behind me to the honking of whoever they cut off.

"I need you to take me to Jersey."

"Not Jersey," I said. "That's not a good idea."

Instead, I turned off at 178th Street and drove beside the bus station where we had another opportunity to move through traffic and pedestrians who didn't care anything about our need to be in a hurry.

"Stop," Viola yelled and grabbed the steering wheel.

"Stupid," I told her and corrected.

I took St. Nicholas and passed the 30th Precinct at 151st, speeding. Nobody noticed and I didn't hear any sirens. But ahead of us I saw police cars at Viola's house. She grabbed the wheel again and I managed to pull the car over to the curb and stop.

I got out and Viola slid over to the driver's seat of the Buick. Ginny got out to move into the front. I tried to stop her.

"Don't go. Stay with us where it's safe," I said to her. "Don't take her," I said to Viola.

"Get in," Viola said and the car was already moving when Ginny jumped into the passenger seat.

They drove away and the Cadillac followed within minutes.

I walked to Viola's house, and when I heard, "Put your hands up," I did.

Captain Obsidian Bailey walked out of the house and he was a welcome presence. He felt like safety, and I knew I had been missing the feeling. My shoulders even dropped a little. But it was only an instant, before I felt the anger taking its place again.

"There is drug money in Viola's Buick, and those men in the red Cadillac who are following her are after the money. It's theirs. And Virginia is in the car."

He said something into his radio.

Then, he said to me, "Pearl, I need you to stand here with me."

He took my hand. "I'm so sorry Pearl," he said.

We watched them rolling Mister Bell into an ambulance.

He was close to dead. But Bobby Bop was all the way dead.

"Do you know who shot Bell?" he asked me.

"Bobby Bop. It looked like he might have been aiming at Viola and Mister Bell got between them," I said.

"And then who killed Bobby Bop?"

"Viola shot him."

EPILOGUE

I was up most of the night at the precinct. I walked the detectives through the replay—the conversation between Viola and her lover partner, and how Viola shot him at the same time the generator exploded. Then the part where Bobby was at the window with his big gun and Mr. Bell was in the alley. And then the car chase. I didn't tell them Al was there.

I gave them positions and we acted out the parts. The acting gave me some welcome distance from the deed. And it moved the energy into the storytelling in my mind and away from my heart.

Obsidian came back to tell me they found the Caddy abandoned under the viaduct by the river. There was no money and no Viola and no Virginia.

He asked me, "How does it feel to be in danger? To witness someone dying? Did you feel tenderness toward your fellow man and fellow woman? Was your heart open?"

I got the point he was making, using the language from my meditation at the precinct.

"No," I said. "I noticed my heart had closed. I disassociated to protect myself."

In the morning in front of the bank, however, my heart did open. I had marched across the street away from the bank and Obsidian because I felt the need to re-establish a safe distance between him and me.

When I turned back I got a wider view of the two lines leading to the bank's covered windows and doors stretching and turning at opposite corners up both Adam Clayton Powell and Frederick Douglass Boulevards. And I felt the incredible tenderness I was talking about and that I practiced for.

My people. Glorious and complex. I remembered Langston Hughes once said, They don't know how beautiful it is to be colored.

"Pearl! Pearl!" Samantha was waving a piece of paper at me as she made her way across the street. She's one of those slow-moving sisters.

"You got another fax from Roger," she said. When she finally got to me, she passed me a single page rolled lengthwise like a baton.

"Thank you, Samantha."

"Sure," she said. "The devil is busy," she added as she turned away without waiting for a reply. I unrolled the paper. It was a poem. I folded it in half.

"Who's Roger?" Obsidian asked from behind me. He had done that thing he does. Sneaking up on a person is probably an essential talent for his cop job.

I turned to him and told half a truth. "Roger is my friend who teaches kickboxing and mixed martial arts to my meditators."

"I wish the brother well," he said. "But you're going to be spending a lot of time in the City. And I don't think you can be trusted."

I deserved that but I didn't expect it.

"If I'm going to be here, I need to meditate with your people," I said. "That was hard last night."

"You watched Bobby Bop get shot. Did you feel the danger? Did you feel the chemicals your body unleashed?"

"Yes. If you're talking about fear and grief, I felt all of it."

"So, my people experience that all the time and their intention is to protect themselves from a danger they perceive will leave them dead in the street."

"Perception is framing reality—figuring out how we think things are," I said. "You say your police perceive danger in the dark bodies they're supposed to protect. Do you hear yourself?"

"I'm not afraid. This is my community. But we can't afford empathy and an open heart. That kind of connection will get in the way of us doing our job. You saw how fast that happened last night. You won't have to worry about meditating at the precinct again. It's not going to happen."

"This morning I sat with the direct experience of being activated and being aware of where the reaction was landing in my body. I could tolerate it barely and stay present to my thoughts and feelings and watch them change. Like being on a desert and seeing an oasis in the distance and the possibility of release from a terrible thirst. Then getting there and taking the water to my lips. That one moment of tasting freedom. I could do it because I practice."

"I practice too. I discharged by moving by body this morning."

"But we can't just discharge the grief and rage. To heal, we have to admit to what's happening—to the fact that the community and the cops are all being triggered again and again without release."

"Them and us. That's the place we never step out from," he said.

"My practice offers the experience of finding refuge and also of awakening from the illusion of separation," I said. I pulled out my notebook. "Tell me again about how your black mayor and black police commissioner will have you getting out of your cars and walking the streets."

"I'm not talking about this with you. I came to tell you I got a call. Viola is in custody. They were stopped at LaGuardia. Virginia asked you to come get her. I'll be back for you."

I watched him walk away.

Other police on horses clopped down the boulevard in front of the restive crowd.

"Save the bank! Save the bank!"

Finally, belatedly, the crowd began chanting loud, like they meant it.

The bank doors had opened. The line moved, and Adrianne walked into the bank with the first in line.

She came back out and turned down her thumb to let me know they were cutting checks.

We were right, and, as she turned back to the line, she raised her fist in an incongruous power salute. I gave it back to her.

Who Shot John?

C H A P T E R · 1

(Monday)

I pulled down a hat to hide under in case Lt. Peace Knight, action figure, might be recognized by my Harlem neighbors as I was going about my business—the business of Pearl Washington, actor, and daughter of Harlem.

Lt. Knight had just solved a couple of crimes in the third movie in the Harlem Knight series. As much as I enjoyed finally shooting a Harlem Knight movie in Harlem, it did not make a significant difference in the tired familiarity of playing the same role again. This was getting old.

As I walked down Seventh Avenue, Adam Clayton Powell, Jr. Blvd., my memories of my hometown were refracted by the way the changes hit the familiar. And it was even more disorienting because Harlem had turned into a ghost town, a netherworld that I walked through from 135th Street.

Where was everybody?

When I got to 125th Street, I found them.

The streets were full. But the shops were empty behind the metal gates that were still rolled down, most of them displaying the dancing, strutting images painted by Franco the Great. Because even the store owners who are not know it's a black thing.

The police and the shopkeepers were mostly talking to each other.

The population of peddlers and vendors who usually sell oils and books and dolls and hats and music and things along both sides of Martin Luther King Jr., Blvd. were standing around or pacing in their work clothes—African jalabas, yards of skirt, Malcolm X and Che t-shirts, khakis and cargo pants and jeans. They had not been allowed to set up.

The journalists were the ones doing most of the moving from one group to the next, breaking the borders that separated the tribes, shoving microphones and video cameras in front of faces.

I took off my hat, folded it in my hand and checked the barrette at my neck before I walked over to stand behind the television cameraman. Karl had provided still photographs when I was running my father's newspaper four years ago, and he had moved from the newspaper business to television. Knowing Karl, his camera was no doubt sweeping the wide boulevard and the Apollo theater to capture a panorama for an establishing shot of Harlem in 1994.

Then he zoomed in on a close-up of television newsman John Johnson where he was standing ready to interview a shopkeeper. Karl gave the sign. Show time.

"They put Krazy Glue in our locks," said the owner of the men's clothing store we were standing in front of.

"That's why you are still closed?" John asked. "I thought you were afraid to open because you expected some violence. Although you certainly have enough police protection."

"I'm not afraid to be here. I'm never afraid to be here. I've been here for years. Everybody knows me. I pay taxes. They don't pay taxes."

"They put their carts right in front of my store," another man said and he pointed to the sneaker store next door.

"Where would you have them put their carts?" John asked.

He looked surprised. "Somewhere else. Not right on the sidewalk at my door."

I felt the beating drums as much as I heard them, and when I turned, I saw the street vendors marching. The interruption they provided was perfect for the piece Karl and John were creating.

A chorus of voices chanted:

"If we can't eat; they won't eat."

"Whose streets? Our streets?"

"Harlem is for Africans. At home and abroad."

"No justice; no peace."

"Racist Giuliani got to go."

They were old people and kids, men and women. They came from continental Africa and the West Indies and New Jersey, Brooklyn and the Bronx and 111th Street. Not everyone marched, but there was a substantial parade. Some were rolling their folded tables and plaid bags of inventory along with them. Many had arrived without their moveable shops, and had come ready to fight back this morning. The man who was their leader was in front with a phalanx of other familiar allies. But no elected officials that I recognized were in the street or on the sidewalks. Missing in action.

Karl was shooting the marchers. He was walking backwards, panning, actually kneeling in the street so they marched around him. They were an army of color, probably 200 strong, threading its way east across 1-2-5 through a gauntlet. So much anger and no small amount of fear showed on their faces.

Some of the same emotions were on the faces of more than 400 policemen from all over the city who were standing poised along the route. They included community affairs cops in their blue windbreakers and commanders in their dark suits and white shirts. Some were on horses, some were in riot gear, expecting what? I wondered.

I marched with them on the sidewalk and turned with them at Seventh Avenue toward 126th Street and the plaza at the Adam Clayton Powell, Jr. State Office Building.

There was a soundtrack like there always is on Martin Luther King, Jr. Blvd.

And it took a few beats to confirm it was not the bass from Eric B. & Rakim but gunshots I was hearing suddenly and echoing out into the big sky,

John was on his knees. I ran over to him.

"Where were you hit?" I asked him and looked to see.

He handed me his notebook before I got pushed out of the way.

"Come with me," Karl said.